**Is that an earthquak**

Imagine a WWII super soldier and his unit were trapped in cutlery by the government, and the only way they could transform back was by being intimate with a woman . . .

Shortly after moving to a new city, Mercedes buys a set of antique silverware from an estate sale and discovers she has a preference for one particular fork. Is the man who appears when the fork disappears real or a salacious fantasy?

If he is real, is he crazy, or could he actually be what he claims to be?

Are you open-minded enough to accept him as he is?

*And fall in love with a fork?*

Find out how far Mercedes will go to save him and his friends in SPOONED and KNIFED.

Cautionary warning:

The spicy scenes in this story are purely fictional. Please do not attempt to re-enact any of them at home. I don't want to hear that my readers FAFO (Forked Around and Found Out). Tines hurt. Let's keep the forks on the table where they belong.

# FORKED

## A Lighthearted Utensil Romance
### Book 1

## Ruth Cardello

### Author Contact
website: RuthCardello.com
email: rcardello@ruthcardello.com
Facebook: Author Ruth Cardello
Twitter: RuthieCardello

# Copyright

## This story is dedicated to:

my teenage daughter who helped me plot all but the spicy scenes. I couldn't have done this without you, Serenity.

my eldest daughter, who brought my vision for the cover alive with her photography skills. I'm so proud of you, Alisha.

my hubby who instantly knew which silverware we needed for the cover. He borrowed his mother's 1940s silver wedding set, and the photo shoots began. I hope your mother is looking down and smiling at the journey her cutlery has taken.

my friends who didn't question my sanity when I proposed the plot of this book. Thank you for never tiring of discussing plot points or sharing in the giddy enjoyment of watching the story take form. One was so helpful I named a cat after him.

**Trigger warning:**
This novella is about a World War II super soldier, trapped inside a fork, who can only take human form again by being intimate with a woman. It also contains some violence.

## Note to my readers

You may ask yourself: "How does an author go from writing romances about billionaires to utensils?" I could try to come up with a funny response to the question, but here's the truth . . .

I'm the youngest of eleven children. My parents have been gone for over a decade. Last year, I lost another one of my siblings and it was hard. Very hard.

I read a silly book about a door, and it made me laugh during a time when I was finding it difficult to. I told my youngest daughter about the book (not the details, just the premise). She joked that I should write about something as ridiculous. Since we were out to eat, she suggested a fork romance. We laughed until we were holding our sides as we came up with the perfect backstory of how a man might become a fork.

And, of course, he had to be someone spectacular when he reverted back to being a man.

I have laughed every single time I sat down to write this book and the process has been good for my soul. It's not a story that's meant to be taken seriously. I wrote it to help me find my smile again and I hope it lifts the moods of those who read it.

# Chapter One

*Mercedes*

*Providence, Rhode Island*
*2024*

T ODAY IS THE day.

It's now or never.

I take a deep, fortifying breath and step into the elevator after someone who is quite arguably the most attractive man in all of Rhode Island. Tall and lean with a mop of curls, perfect teeth, and a better sense of style than I've ever had. He nods at me, and I nearly lose my nerve.

The smile I flash him is meant to be warm and welcoming, but considering how nervous I am, I'm sure it appears pained, because he quickly looks away. I turn so, like him, I'm facing the elevator door and remind myself if I don't shoot my shot there's a one hundred percent certainty he'll never notice me.

Twenty-three rides in the elevator together. Eight with

several other tenants. Six with one other person. Nine with just me. Zero interaction other than a nod in greeting.

I've watched him since he moved in. Okay, that sounds bad. It's not like I stalk him or anything like that. I moved to Providence right before the pandemic and work from home, so suffice it to say, I don't have a busy social calendar. Yes, the world has reopened, and a lot of people have gone back to what some might call normal, but I didn't start out as much of an extrovert and will admit that having an excuse to stay home alone was a relief for a long time.

If I wanted to see no one and do nothing, though, I could have stayed on Block Island. Except for the summer, it's a pretty quiet place. Even quieter, for me, after my parents moved south for the warmer weather right after I graduated from college.

It took a while for me to find the courage to relocate on my own, but moving to Providence to meet people just before the world closed down was what I would call classic Mercedes timing.

But my luck is about to change.

I'm taking charge of my life and my happiness.

I gulp in air as the door to the elevator closes. He lives on the fourth floor, which means I don't have much time to do this. "Hi, I'm Mercedes," I say breathlessly.

"Hi," he answers in a friendly tone.

I can do this.

I clear my throat. "I know you don't know me, but I see

you ride your bike on weekends and tomorrow is Saturday. I have a bike. It's in storage, but I could get it out, and I was thinking we could go for a ride together sometime."

"Sure," he answers without looking at me.

Sure? Just like that. "Okay. Okay. When would you like to do this? Tomorrow?"

"That sounds good."

*That sounds good.* Oh, my God, did he just say yes to tomorrow? I'm too excited to look at him in case he can see giddiness in my eyes. "It's a date, then."

"Listen, I'm in the elevator and not alone, so let's bang out the details via email. Sure. Sounds good. I'll have that to you by Monday."

What?

Who is he talking to?

Heat warms my face. Not me—that's who. He's on the phone. Did he hear anything I said?

My gaze flies to the lit floor number. Fantastic. It only took me two floors to humiliate myself. Perfect. Hopefully, the ride of shame back down to my floor will be a solo one.

The elevator stops on the fourth floor, and he pauses before exiting. For just a moment, he meets my gaze with a confused expression. "I'm sorry, did you say something to me a moment ago? I was on a call."

"No." My answer comes out in a strangled tone.

"Oh, okay. I wasn't sure. I thought I heard your voice in the background."

If it were possible to die simply by wanting to, I would have dropped into a heap of dead at his feet. "No."

He blocks the door from closing with his hand. "Are you okay?"

Only because I have to say something, I blurt, "I have your mail."

"My mail?"

"It was put in my box by accident."

His smile transforms his face, and my breath catches in my throat. "And you want to return it to me? That's so nice. Thanks. See, this is exactly why I chose a small city to move to. I want to be part of a community that watches out for each other."

"Yeah."

"I'm Greg." His lopsided grin is adorable. "But you already know that, I guess, if you have my mail."

I nod.

"Should I drop by to get it? You're also welcome to bring it by my place. I'm in 414."

"Yes." I shake my head. "I mean, I'll bring it to you."

He flashes another smile. "Thanks. I'd really appreciate that." He steps out and the door between us closes.

*Shit, now I have to steal some of his mail.*

# Chapter Two

Ⅲ

## *Mercedes*

A SHORT TIME later, I place a dish of food in front of my roommate. It's against my lease to have a pet, so on paper Mike is a twenty-five-year-old grad student at Brown University with good credit and great references. In reality, he's an orange tabby of unknown age who followed me home shortly after I moved to Providence. With half of one ear missing and covered with fleas, I thought he'd be grateful for a bath and medical attention. Gratitude isn't something Mike is big on.

I know I should make him eat on the floor, but since he is often the only one I speak to, he deserves a spot at the table. Tonight's fare? A mix of high-end canned food and boneless, skinless chicken strips. He meows at me, and I ask myself for the hundredth time if I should invest in the communication buttons that I keep seeing on social media.

No. I'm a worst-case scenario contemplator. If I can't handle how something could go wrong, I don't do it.

What if those death glares he sometimes gives me are real? I prefer to let his criticisms of me only happen in my imagination.

According to my parents, I always hyper-analyzed everything. I crawled longer than the doctors thought I should have because falling looked painful. Toilet training was terrifying as soon as I imagined what would happen if my bare bottom touched the water and I was sucked away by an accidental flush. Don't even get me started on how I could have turned twenty-four and still not have had sex with anyone.

Have you seen photos of what venereal diseases can do to a woman's labia? If you haven't, save yourself and don't because it only leads down a rabbit hole of treatment options and photos that still haunt me years after viewing them.

Those images are part of why I'm still a virgin. But I have to put them behind me.

I mean, crawling hadn't been a lifelong option.

I've conquered my fear of toilets.

How difficult could it be to fuck someone?

I've already chosen the man. Mr. Room 414.

Mike meows at me when I leave the table to retrieve my own dinner. He's judging me. "I'm glad I can't understand you," I say. "I don't want you to talk me out of this plan."

On my way to the table I stop and retrieve my favorite fork from the dishrack beside the sink. I have an entire case of silverware and have never cared much about which utensil I use, but there's something special about this fork. It's old-fashioned and sterling silver. Perfectly weighted with solid tines that feel good in my mouth.

People don't make quality like this anymore, which is why, when I came across the case of silverware at an estate sale, I bought it. Sure, a fancy setting for six wasn't a practical investment for a woman who lives alone and never entertains, but circumstances can change.

I could drop something in the hallway and strike up a conversation with a group of five people who find me hilarious. They'll invite me over for a meal and things will go so well that I'll return the favor. Entertaining possible new best friends shouldn't be done with plastic utensils.

I place my fork beside my plate of chicken and sit down. As I use the side of the fork to cut my food, I consider getting up to retrieve a knife, but I've become used to using only the fork. I stab a piece of meat and bring it to my mouth with anticipation. Prior to owning this set, I didn't understand how different sterling silver would feel from stainless steel.

It's heavier and warmer, somehow making the act of eating something as simple as plain chicken feel like an indulgence. I love the way it feels on my lips and how it slides over my tongue.

Holding the fork in one hand, I meet my cat's gaze. "This is why I have to have sex with someone, Mike. I'm beginning to find inanimate objects sexy. I watched a video once about some guy who found his car attractive—really, really attractive. Clearly, he was mentally ill." I chuckle, then sober and look at the fork. "I like this fork, but I don't *like* this fork. Sure, it's my favorite, but I could probably mix it up with the other forks and not know the difference. I like the feel of expensive cutlery, that's all."

I make the mistake of meeting Mike's gaze again. He thinks he's better than I am, but he's not. "You lick what's left of your balls on my pillow when you think I'm not looking so let's be kinder when it comes to judging each other, okay?"

He flicks his tail dismissively.

"I'm going to have a normal life," I say defensively. "I'm going to get out there, get to know people, maybe sleep around a little, and have friends who call me at all hours because they can't wait until morning to share their news with me. I'm so close to having that life. I'm just working myself up to actually having conversations with people."

I exchange another look with Mike. "So, I asked Greg out today. The guy from upstairs. And before you ask, it went badly." I take another bite of chicken, savoring the fork more than the meat before saying, "But when life closes an elevator door it opens a mailbox."

I snort laugh.

Mike swishes his tail in annoyance.

"Sorry, of course you don't understand. He didn't hear me because he was on a call. I didn't notice. So, yeah, that was painful. But, I told him I have his mail so now if I can figure out how to get some, I'll have an excuse to go upstairs to see him. And he was adorably grateful." I sigh. "I wish I'd said I have something of his that would be easier to get. I could tell him I lost his mail." I snap my fingers. "Or that you shredded it. No, wait, he can't know about you until I'm sure I can trust him."

I look down at the cat hair on my shirt and gasp. "What if he's allergic to you?" I shake my head. "No. I'm not doing this. I refuse to overthink myself right into another year of virginity."

The fork in my hand vibrates.

Or my reaction to the idea of another birthday coming and going alone is so strong that my hand won't stop shaking.

No, it's the fork moving.

I drop it to the table.

It stops moving. Of course it does, because forks don't do anything on their own.

Until it starts moving again.

Oh, my God, this is an earthquake. I've never been in one.

But the floor isn't moving.

And nothing else in the room is.

Just the fork.

Maybe earthquakes in New England are so subtle I don't realize the whole building is shaking.

Mike whips the fork away from me and off the other side of the table. "Mike," I say in reprimand then bend, hoping I can retrieve the fork from my side. If this is an earthquake, being under the table is supposed to be safer, isn't it?

Maybe Mike was trying to save my life. Good kitty. He does love me.

I duck beneath the table for the fork but don't see it. Damn. As I begin to back out from beneath the table I see a pair of well-polished leather shoes. I straighten in surprise. The sound of my head cracking against the table echoes through the room and I swear. Pain blurs my vision. Mike appears beside me and, as usual, is absolutely no help.

I don't know anyone who wears shiny shoes. Not Greg. Not the maintenance men. Did I leave the door of my apartment open or did someone just break in?

Am I being robbed by someone in dress shoes? There's no way the intruder doesn't know I'm there. I look around for my fork. A knife would be better to stab someone with, but something is better than nothing.

The fork is nowhere to be seen.

So much for my luck changing.

I breathe and attempt to calm myself. The pants above the shiny shoes are neatly creased. What kind of criminal irons his pants? Even Mr. Room 414 doesn't and he's fancy.

Slowly, I shift so I can peer over the edge of the table. I must have hit my head harder than I thought because as my gaze rises, the chance of what I'm looking at being real decreases. Pressed khaki pants are topped by an olive, belted, uniform jacket with a large number of medals on it. I swallow hard. I'm hallucinating—a side effect from a concussion? How quickly does that happen?

The man has a broad chest, thick muscular neck, chiseled jaw, and the kind of piercing blue eyes that pull a person in and hold them captive. His hair is cut short and neat. My bruised brain has good taste.

His voice is several octaves deeper than the man upstairs when he says, "You're not at all how I imagined you."

I groan and lift myself to a standing position. "Really? Brain damage can produce a gorgeous man but not one who's attracted to me?"

"Ma'am, are you hurt?"

Lord, his voice is sexy. Masculine and demanding. Everything about him is hard and seasoned. This is the kind of man other men would make way for if he walked through a crowd. Dangerous. Rough.

What's with the outdated uniform? Is he into cos play? I could dig that.

I touch the now sensitive spot on the back of my head. "Am I dead? That makes sense. There really was an earthquake, but instead of saving me the table crushed me. And you're my spirit guide to the other side." I look around in panic. "Did Mike make it or is he dead too?"

The gorgeous military apparition frowns at me. "Who's Mike?"

"My cat."

He looks around. "This isn't heaven. For a while there, I thought it might be, but this—this is definitely somewhere else."

"You're dead too?"

"I don't believe so."

"So, you're not here to guide me to the light?"

"Correct."

"Well, I'm not going in the other direction. I'm sure of that. I don't sin. I mean, I don't do enough of anything to warrant going anywhere but to the light. Okay, so I lied today. And I was plotting to steal. But in the scheme of things, how bad is that? And as far as purity. You don't get purer than me. I haven't so much as gone down on a man and some people don't even consider that sex, but I always did. So absolute virgin here. That has to count for something."

A corner of his mouth lifts as if he's amused. "Duly noted, but not information that is currently productive. Who are you?"

"Wait, hold on. If I'm not dead, I'm unconscious. I can deal with that. I'm unconscious and under the table. All I have to do is wake myself up." I slap my face lightly on one side and then the other. "Wake up, Mercedes. You have friends to make, a guy to fuck, and a cat to care for. Wake up."

The man in the olive uniform looks around and then settles those amazing blue eyes back on me. "What year is it?"

"Time-traveling delusion. That's where we're taking this? Okay, brain, I see you're struggling, but that's better than a gorgeous stranger who doesn't find me attractive. Is this like a puzzle I have to solve to wake up?"

"Sure. What year is it?"

"Twenty twenty-four."

"And where are we?"

"In my apartment in Providence, Rhode Island."

"Did we win against Japan?"

I shrug. "Win?"

"World War II."

Not sure why I'm fantasizing about a soldier when I've never even stayed awake through an entire war movie, but I'm willing to play along to wake up. "We did. We dropped a bomb on Japan and that pretty much ended the war."

"What kind of bomb?"

"An atomic one."

He sways on his feet, then steadies himself by holding on to the back of a chair. "We were told that would never happen."

# Chapter Three

*Hugh*

*London, May 8
1945*

WE'VE WON THE war—at least this part of it. Germany surrendered. Churchill declared today a public holiday. People are dancing in the streets, and every Allied soldier is being heralded as a hero.

Except my unit. Our existence and participation in supporting our military is top-tier classified information. We knew when we signed on that there'd be no fame for us and that was okay.

I glance at the white line that rings the base of my trigger finger. For each of the twelve men at my table, the shame of staying behind when all able-bodied men enlisted and deployed far outweighed the fear of the unknown.

Inhaling sharply, I take a moment to appreciate the recognition of our success. Director Falcon invited us to the

Savoy Hotel for a swanky dinner honoring our latest mission. Despite the small number of people in attendance, it is a formal affair during which everyone in my unit was awarded a chest full of medals. There is a sense of anticipation since we were told our time with the program would end in exactly this way.

I look down the long table at what is left of the men who became my family. Together, we've risked, risen, survived, and achieved—and together, we'll remember and mourn those of us who won't be going home after the war. The crisp white linen and place settings are fancy enough for royalty and I'm sure I'm not the only one who feels out of place.

Fresh from the field, we washed off the grime of a week without shelter or shower, bandaged our wounds, and donned the pressed dress uniforms of a military we were not officially members of. All for what? Is the Inkwell Project coming to an end?

Or is this the beginning of a new phase of it?

The neck of my uniform is uncomfortably tight. I tuck a finger beneath the knot of my tie and loosen it a hair. Unlike some of the men in the unit, I didn't break the rules or indulge in vigilantism. Everything I did was by direct order and with the goal of world peace. If unchecked, the German scientists would develop a bomb with a power unlike anything the world had ever seen.

So, under the veil of night, we lured and kidnapped

many of the greatest minds in Germany. Many with their families. Those we determined uncooperative haunted me. We released no one. Anyone we encountered either joined the Allied Forces voluntarily or was handed over to the director—along with anyone who was taken with them.

We were told it was a necessary evil and I have to believe there was no other way. The world was not ready for an atomic bomb. Neither side. What we did, however ugly, we did for all of humanity.

Even if I could go home, I don't want to. It's not an option, though, because to them, we're already dead. It had to be that way because we're all now physically different in ways we could never hide or explain to those who knew us.

However, if the past few years taught us anything, it was how to rise in the face of a challenge. Nothing is impossible. Will we be sent across the ocean together or separated and dispersed? Either way, we will continue to use our talents and strengths for good.

Waiters refill our glasses with water and serve bowls of clear soup, which only someone who never knew hunger would consider a first-course reward for heroism. The man to my left accepts it with gratitude beyond what I feel. From day one, Jack was more optimistic than the rest of us. Tall and built like a tank, he's a gentle giant who somehow still has a love of humanity despite all we've seen. His smile reaches his oddly colored eyes. They're green but with brown and white specks around each iris. "If this is the end, do you think they'll let us out to celebrate? I hear every dogface will have a sweetheart tonight."

"Is that what you have on your mind?" I joke.

"Always," Jack replies without missing a beat.

The soldier directly across from us, Ray, interjects, "We've earned it, wouldn't you say? Let the good times roll on in."

Never one to be left out of a joke, Pete adds, "I'm hoping for a more athletic romp than a roll, but honestly, I'll happily accept whatever's offered."

"I'm ready for some R&R," I say with a smile and shake my head.

"The rest of us are happy enough with one, but of course, Hugh wants two. Let me guess. Rebecca and Rose?" Jack asks, and the rest of us laugh.

"I didn't know Rose was your mother's name," Ray tosses in with a snicker.

The entire table goes silent.

Jack rises to his feet.

I do as well. Jack only has one fuse guaranteed to set him off and that is any mention of his family. Unlike some of us, they were close and being away from them is difficult for him. "Hey, there, buddy. Ray never thinks before he speaks. He's already sorry he said it. Right, Ray?"

"Sure," Ray said.

It isn't enough. Jack's chest puffs and his fists clench at his side. I lay a hand on his shoulder. "We've been through too much together and have too much to celebrate to do this. Come on, Ray, we don't need any guff today."

Ray stands and holds out a hand to Jack. "Sorry, Jack. I didn't mean anything by it."

Jack visibly relaxes and shakes Ray's hand before we all retake our seats.

Deciding it's best to remind them of the reasons we made it as far as we have, I say, "If this is the end, I'm going to miss blowing shit up."

From a few seats down, Edward pipes up. "You can say that even though a mine nearly killed you?"

My back flexes automatically as I remember the hot shrapnel slicing through my muscles. There's no pain or residual tightness even though the initial damage was extensive. All that remains is a faint white scar much like the one on my finger. "The first mine is never a person's best," I joke.

Jack sighs and smiles. "My first was amazing. She was twenty years older and divorced. The things that woman taught me . . ."

"Has anyone . . . you know, since joining the program. Have you . . .?" Ray stops and looks around to make sure no one is listening.

"Just my hand," I admit.

Edward leans in and lowers his voice. "I almost did once, but I was afraid to hurt her."

"Wait! Is yours different?" Jack nods toward his crotch.

"Mine's the same."

"Too bad you can't regrow something that was never there." Ray chuckles.

Jack punches me so hard in the shoulder he nearly knocks me out of my chair. "Pass that across to Ray, please."

I lean forward and knock a laughing Ray hard enough in the chest that the chair tips back before he rights it.

"Hey!"

I shrug. "He said *please*."

The director calls our attention to the front of the room again. He thanks us for our dedication to the program then pauses. "One day Project Inkwell will no longer be a secret and when that day comes, all of you will be remembered as the heroes you are. The sacrifices you made will not be forgotten."

Jack whispers, "If by sacrifice he means we're all supposed to return to our rooms alone tonight, I say we sneak out. They can't stop all of us, and forgiveness is easier to gain than permission."

"I'm with you on that," Ray agrees.

Edward doesn't look as sure. "We don't know what comes next. Shouldn't we wait to see what's being offered before we blow our chance at what could be a piece-of-cake assignment?"

Partying with all of London and half the world is tempting. I understand Edward's concerns, but we'll never be in this situation again and it's been too long since I've been with a woman. As the normally levelheaded one, it's often my vote that sways the group. So, although I'm leaning toward Jack's plan, I don't want to move forward recklessly. "Don't talk about it here. We'll return to our rooms, change into something less likely to catch anyone's attention and do this right. Edward is correct that we need to be careful. And not just regarding getting caught. We're stronger than we used to be. And different in ways we might not yet know. I've watched some of you change color while you sleep. Don't drink. Don't get sloppy. Be sober. Be kind."

Edward motions for me to stop talking and pay attention. I freeze then follow his gaze. We're alone. The director is gone. The waitstaff is as well. There's an eerie calm like one that happens just before lightning strikes.

I rise to my feet. The rest of the unit does as well.

Ray says something that sounds like an apology.

A flash blinds me and then there's nothing.

## *Hugh*

*Providence, Rhode Island*
*2024*

NOTHING, THAT IS, until the first time I felt her touch. Sometimes warm and comforting. Sometimes hot and wet. The scent and taste of her filled my senses until it felt as if we were one. Time became irrelevant. There was only her and the absence of her.

The small brunette before me has eyes as wild as her hair and clothing so baggy I might have confused her with the opposite sex. Despite looking disheveled, she appears clean. I look around her tidy living space. There are some items I don't recognize, but the hiss from the orange cat on the table is familiar.

Dogs love me.

Cats not so much.

Once, on a dare, I paid a circus psychic fifty cents for a reading. She warned me to stay away from the lion cage because the past and the future are intertwined, and cats can sense the supernatural. She also told me to remember that if I chose to regain something I had yet to lose, the price would be losing everything I knew.

I laughed off the nonsense, but if the woman before me isn't lying, eighty years has passed since the award dinner I attended in London. I flex my right hand. It's as it was back then, right down to the white line at the base of my trigger finger.

What happened back in London?

Where's the rest of my unit?

Why am I in Rhode Island?

My attention returns to the brunette before me. She definitely doesn't look anything like I imagined the woman I was addicted to experiencing.

"Come here," I command.

Her eyes widen and she sputters something incomprehensible while shaking her head.

I close the distance between us and take her chin firmly in one hand. "I need to know."

She attempts to move away, but I hold her in place and swoop down for a taste.

The moment our lips touch, the questions swirling through my head cease to matter. Everything beyond her fades away until she feels necessary for my very existence. I close my eyes, tease her lips to open for mine, and plunder her sweet mouth.

Her hands grip my shoulders, and the sounds she makes nearly sends me to the place she asked if I was there to guide her to. It's too much and not nearly enough all at once. I yank myself away from her and wipe a hand across my mouth angrily.

She's shaking like a Chihuahua, and I don't know if I should apologize or demand she release me from whatever spell she has me under.

# Chapter Four

*Mercedes*

*Providence, Rhode Island*
*2024*

SO THAT JUST happened.

I kissed a figment of my imagination and liked it. Really liked it. It was a *I'm-not-sure-I-can-ever-find-another-man-attractive-after-that kind of kiss.*

I'm losing my mind.

Mike meows at me from the tabletop again. I laugh nervously and sit down. "If I'm not dead, and I'm not unconscious, then this is a mental breakdown." I pick up my phone and search for what a person should do if they start hallucinating. The first suggestion is to call a doctor. Possible causes? Epilepsy. Never had a history of that. Parkinson's. I don't know enough about that to know if I have it. Schizophrenia. A chronic, severe mental disorder that affects the way a person thinks, expresses themselves, perceives reality and relates to others . . .

That's not inconceivable—

"What is that thing?" asks the soldier I hoped would disappear if I ignored him.

"It's my phone."

He bends to look over my shoulder. "That's not like any phone I've ever seen."

I take a deep breath. "I would take the time to explain it to you, but what I really need to focus on right now is how to stop being able to see and hear you."

"And your little machine can tell you that?"

"The internet knows everything." Hands shaking, I type in how to stop a panic attack. "At least, I hope so."

"The internet? What is it and how does it work?"

Maybe explaining it to him will help me calm. That has to be the first step to making a hallucination go away. Then, once he's gone, I'll find a good doctor. Or maybe this is a one-time event no one will ever need to hear about. "This is a little computer."

"A computer? That small?"

"Yes. And it's connected through the air to computers all around the world that share information." If we're still doing the whole time-travel thing, I guess I can play along. "What time period are you from?"

"I was born in 1920."

I swallow hard. "Sure. And you're now—"

"Twenty-five."

"Me too. Not really. I'm twenty-*four*, not five." I let out a nervous laugh and a fact. "September 2, 1945. That's when World War II ended."

"September? And it ended with the dropping of an atomic bomb?"

"Two actually." I grimace, do a quick search for how World War II ended then turn the phone for him to read it.

He does then says, "More. What happened next?"

"Just swipe up."

He gives me a long look.

I move my finger across the screen and show him. That's all it takes for him to scan the rest of the page about the end of the war.

"Look up Project Inkwell," he demands.

I frown. "You're pushy for someone I'm imagining."

The smile he flashes me holds no warmth. "Do it."

I search then show him the results. "You're interested in learning how to express yourself through writing?"

He shakes his head and growls, "Look again. Reference World War II."

"Nothing. The Manhattan Project keeps coming up. Some atomic bomb testing in Mexico in July of 1945."

"Show me."

I give him a pointed look that he doesn't appear to understand at first.

Until he does. "Please," he says impatiently.

I hand him the phone, not sure it won't simply drop to

the floor but it doesn't. He reads, swipes for more, then reads the article to the end. He stops and looks at me. "How do I ask it something?"

"You type your question in the search bar or you can ask it aloud." I touch the speaker icon. "If you touch this."

"Where is Hugh Emerson?" he says louder than necessary into the phone. "None of these are me." He presses the microphone icon again and says, "Where is Jack Sully?" Looking more frustrated with each name he searches for until he tosses the phone back to me. I catch it, then hold it to my chest.

"Who are those people?"

"People who might know what happened to me. I don't understand any of this. Why am I here? *How* am I here? Where is everyone else?" He searches my face. "I know you. You've been part of whatever this is for a while now. How? Where was I until a few minutes ago and how were you connected to me?"

I put my phone in my sweatpants' side pocket and raise my hands in surrender. "I don't know what you're talking about. I never met you before today and, honestly, I'm still trying to figure out if you're real."

He looms over me and takes one of my hands in his. I'm both terrified and more than a little turned on. "I know your hand." He runs a thumb across my bottom lip. "I know your mouth. The taste of you. The feel of you. I crave it. Why?"

My voice sounds strangled as I say, "I must be asleep on

the couch and this is all a dream. Thankfully I live alone so there's no one to judge me if I wake up humping one of the cushions."

His eyebrows arch then lower. "You're an odd woman."

I swallow hard. "And you're not living up to the fantasy part of this. This is *my* sex dream. Shouldn't you say nice things to me?"

He drops my hand. "How did I get here?"

I shrug. "You just appeared."

"*Poof?* Like that?"

"Yes." I blink a few times. "No, not exactly. I was eating, and my fork started vibrating. I thought it was an earthquake. I dropped the fork. Mike threw it on the floor. I hate when he does that. And I was looking for it when I saw you."

He searches the area. "I don't see a fork on the floor."

"It's there—somewhere. Forks don't just magically disappear."

"No, they don't." He shakes his head. "Yesterday, did you lick the entire length of the fork?"

"No," I deny automatically even though a memory of doing exactly that comes back to me.

He buries a hand in my hair, pulls me closer, and tips my head back, so I'm forced to meet his gaze. "Don't lie to me."

My entire body starts humming for his. Damn, this dream is good. "Would you punish me if I did?"

His nostrils flare. "Answer the question."

"Yes. Yes, I licked the handle of the fork. I was using it to eat ice cream, and some dripped onto my fingers." I ran my tongue across my bottom lip. "I know I should use a spoon, but there's something about that fork. Everything tastes better on it."

His grip on my hair tightens. "Where did you get the fork?"

"At an estate sale."

"Was it alone or in a set?"

"A set."

"Where is it?"

"The fork? I told you. It's on the floor somewhere."

"No, the rest of the silverware. Show it to me."

He releases me. The absence of his touch has me feeling like a deflating balloon. This is truly the strangest dream I've ever had. I lead him toward my kitchenette and to the velvet-lined wooden box I'd left the rest of the silverware in. He picks up the box and holds it to read a small brass label on the front of it. "Inkwell."

"That's the name of the project you asked me to look up."

"Yes."

He places the box down, opens it, and studies its contents. "This is the silverware we used at the award ceremony. I remember thinking how unnecessarily fancy it was."

"What award ceremony?"

He shook his head rather than answering me then looked at his right hand. "None of this seems possible, but I've *seen* impossible—and become it. I don't understand how this happened or if anyone else survived, but I will find out." He closes the box. "And you're going to help me."

# Chapter Five

## *Hugh*

*Boston, Massachusetts*
*1941*

S TANDING IN FRONT of an unmarked door of a storage building in a less savory section of Boston, I retrieve a paper from my pocket and unfold it. It is a flier with a fierce looking eagle descending for attack on it, wings spread wide and proud, but with one leg instead of two.

Uncle Sam needs every bird in the air.

Support the troops by learning a specialized skill.

With your help, they will be invincible. Sign up today to save the world.

No address, but directions to this building and this door.

I use my middle finger to press the doorbell beside the warehouse's alley entrance and don't allow myself the luxury of second-guessing if this is a good decision. The alternative is unacceptable. Every single one of my friends has already gone to fight the war.

The only men left in my town are the very young, the very old, and those like me—the ones who have something wrong with them. My mother tried to tell me I was lucky, but my father understood. Being forty-four years old, even he registered for the draft, and said he was proud to have survived the First World War. My mother didn't understand how pride can overshadow fear. I was more afraid of being left behind than dying. And I wasn't alone with that feeling. Young and old were lying about their ages to qualify to go.

Sadly, I couldn't lie about something I couldn't hide— my missing appendage. Had I known as a child that deciding to cut down a tree on my own would one day cost me the chance to save the world, I would have never picked up that axe.

One missing finger.

It shouldn't have been enough for the Army to classify me as 4-F, unfit for service due to physical reasons.

Because I lacked one finger? In every other way I was strong and healthy. Growing up, I left school early to help support my family. I worked on farms, in factories, doing just about anything that kept food on my parents' table. With more jobs opening every day, my sister was now also working. Dad would soon be sending back his military pay. My family would be fine without me. In a lengthy note I left on the kitchen table, I did my best to explain that I'd send news home as soon as I was able.

The door of the storage building is opened by an expressionless man in an Army officer uniform. I hand him the flier. He nods for me to come inside and closes the door behind me. We make our way down a dim hallway to a room with another officer at a desk.

After I give my name, they don't ask further questions. I get the feeling they already know everything about me.

A tall thin man in civilian clothing appears and greets me with a handshake. He has a stack of papers with him. "This is a top-secret operation," he says. "I can't tell you much until after you've signed on. I can say, though, that it's dangerous. Not everyone will come home."

I stand straighter and hold his gaze. "Will I see battle?"

"Not on the front lines. Our work will be done in the shadows of the war, but it is every bit as essential as firing a bullet. In fact, it may play a larger role in the outcome of the war than any one battle could."

"Which branch of service is this for?"

His lips press together. "Technically, the Army Air Forces. However, due to the sensitive nature of what we'll be tasked to do, your family will need to believe you died before you ship out. It's for their safety as well as yours."

"Only until the end of the war?"

"Of course."

"And what we're doing will support the troops?"

"You'll be heroes."

"Where do I sign?"

# Chapter Six

*Hugh*

*Somewhere in England*
*Four months later*

I N A MUSTY gymnasium of an abandoned school in the outskirts of London, I take my place in the center of a circle of men, many of whom I've come to consider friends. I catch a quick glimpse of my hand, intact again, with just a white circle as a reminder that my trigger finger hadn't always been there. Every man in the room had once felt the shame of not being fit enough for the military. Even our American director lost a leg early in the war and was medically discharged before joining the program. Like us, sitting at home while the world went to hell wasn't something he was willing to accept.

Not all of us made it to England, but we all were told of the risks. Some died immediately after the first injection. They were the lucky ones. They went quickly. Others saw initial good results from the weekly injections. Like the rest of us, their bodies began to regenerate and heal. One man who had severe asthma his whole life had been able to breathe easily again. Something changed, though, halfway through the treatments. Some of us gained increased strength and began to heal faster and with less pain. Those we lost in the second wave went in the opposite direction. They began to deteriorate at a cellular level—slowly and without hope of recovery.

For a while, we each lived in quiet fear that we'd be next, but most of us kept improving. Faster. Stronger. Even our senses became more acute. A deep cut that would have once taken weeks to heal now only took hours.

Supplements were introduced to decrease our need for sleep and increase our attention span. We lost a few more men to madness. One day they seemed normal, the next they attacked someone without provocation.

Those who raised concerns were removed and I have no idea what happened to them. Most of us who remain have secretly agreed to dispose of the supplements rather than take them. The pills went down toilets, into planters, dropped into sewers . . . anywhere but into us.

Our director called us soldiers, but we aren't officially enlisted. Our only fear was dying before we had the chance to fight for our country and the free world.

I look around and say loudly, "Jack."

He joins me in the middle. "Fourteen against two, my

favorite odds."

Combat training with men who could heal meant there were few rules. The last one . . . or two standing won. The prize? Badass bragging rights and the honor of choosing who fought beside him the next day.

Jack isn't the brightest of the bunch. He was born blind and his parents had never sent him to school, but he used his fists like jackhammers and could pulverize even me if I let him close enough. The man has more than his share of bottled rage. I prefer him at my side rather than circling me.

"You're going down today," Franklin jeers from the outer circle. He chose me as his fighting partner earlier in the week and our broken asses were handed to us. I don't blame him for gunning for me now. I should have realized Ray had a weapon on him. Instead of the punch I expected to field from him, Ray stuck me right between the ribs and I hit the floor, leaving Franklin unprotected.

We weren't supposed to bring weapons into the fight circle, but in war, winning is what matters most. I dropped my guard and Ray reminded me that trusting the wrong person could quickly turn deadly.

"Bring it, Frankie." I crouch in preparation of not just him humbling me, but all those around me too, after my win yesterday. This is how we grow stronger. Sparring the unenhanced wasn't a challenge, not when I can lift a car with my bare hands. Outnumbered by men of equal strength keeps us on our toes and at the top of our game. We lose more than we win, but we also fight with a ferocity that one opponent could never inspire.

As if on cue, the circle dissolves into a charge. Back-to-back with Jack, I assess the most vulnerable of those coming for me. Ray boldly takes the first swing. I duck and sweep his legs out from beneath him. As he falls, I grab one of his arms and swing him with all my might. I don't feel bad at all when I hear his arm pop out of its socket. Those to the right of him stumble beneath the force and weight of him being thrown at thcm, which gives me time to address the next threat.

Franklin connects with a flying kick to my chest. One of my ribs cracks audibly, but doesn't pierce a lung. I bounce off Jack's back and use the pain in my chest to my advantage. I unleash thunderous blows one after another on Franklin until he's a bloody heap at my feet, then step over him. *He'll heal.*

Behind me I hear the sound of bodies hitting the floor and bones snapping. I don't turn to see the carnage. Jack has my back. He always does. I'd choose him as a partner every time if I didn't think it would break the morale of the others to always lose to us.

I feel a little bad for my three remaining adversaries. Billy can be taken down every time with a kick to the head. Allen doesn't protect against the second punch. And I don't know how Edward has gotten this far and still hesitates.

I take Billy down first because a good punch from him

cost me a win in the past. Allen doesn't stand a chance because Edward stands back as if politely waiting his turn. I hammer Allen with a few light punches that distract him from the final, powerful blow that snaps his head back and likely breaks his neck.

All that's left is fucking Edward, and I don't want to hit him, but I have to.

He's brilliant, but somehow not smart enough to realize that nice has no place in a war. Nice gets people killed.

I give him a chance to strike me. He does, but not with the force I know he can employ and that pisses me off enough that I give his jaw an upward strike that sends him flying twenty or so feet back.

When I turn, the two I knocked over with Ray are rushing me from the side. I leap and spin, connecting a kick to the side of one of their faces. As he falls, I use him as a step to come down, fists flying on the second one. He lands a few strikes, one to my already broken rib, robbing me of my breath, but I send him to the ground with unrelenting head punches.

Holding my side, I spin to check on Jack's progress. He's standing, legs wide, bloodied hands on his hips with a big-ass grin. "Took you long enough. I almost started to help you."

I touch my side gingerly. *That's going to hurt for the next few hours.* "Come on, let's get everyone some ice."

# Chapter Seven

*Mercedes*

*Providence, Rhode Island*
*2024*

M Y IMAGINARY FRIEND is neither leaving nor showing much interest in me. He's been standing at the window looking at the city for the past fifteen or so minutes. As far as fantasies go, this one is disappointingly uneventful.

Maybe I *should* call a doctor.

Without turning from the window, he says, "I knew cars would be a big thing. I planned on buying one for myself when I came home from the war. Does everyone have one now?"

"Pretty much."

"Jack thought a car would be a poor choice. Horses are . . . *were* cheaper and more reliable."

"Jack?"

"A combat buddy of mine." We're both quiet for a moment, then he asks, "Do you have a horse?"

"No. I rode one once, though. On vacation with my parents. I was scared and didn't want to, but they made me do it anyway. I was so angry with them."

"Are they dead? Your parents."

"No. They're in South Carolina. They wanted to be where the weather is warmer."

"Mine must be long dead—along with everyone I knew."

That's depressing. I pick up Mike and hug him to me. He doesn't protest. "I'm sorry."

"There was no going home to them anyway. Maybe it's better this way."

"I know you're not real, but you're handling being alone better than I would. Pretty much everything scares me."

He glances back at me before returning his attention to the cars below. "The only thing fear ever does is hold a person back."

"Yeah." I pet Mike's head and he rubs against my chin. "That's what my parents told me my whole life. I am who I am, though, and I'm used to never being enough."

He turns fully toward me and my breath catches. The medals on his broad chest sparkle. He's not only taller than Mr. Room 414, but he has a stronger presence. I want to be lifted in the air by him and spun around. I want to be bent over one of those strong arms of his and kissed until it doesn't matter if he's real or not. "I remember that feeling all too well. I wasn't fit to serve in the regular Army, at least that's what my denial paperwork stated—that was a tough time."

"You look healthy."

"I am. Now."

"Wh-what was wrong with you?"

Rather than answering me he walks over and looks down into my eyes. "What's your name?"

"Mercedes. Mercedes Hopper."

"Nice to meet you, Mercedes Mercedes Hopper. My name is Hugh Emerson."

"Those are a lot of medals for a man without a title before his name," I joke. When he doesn't laugh, I ask, "What branch of the military are you in? Were you in?"

"I was never officially enlisted." His eyes darken and he tears one of the medals off and throws it across the room. "And these were only given as a distraction to make sure we were all exactly where they wanted us to be."

"I don't know what you're talking about."

He lifts a hand and caresses one of my cheeks. "You don't have to, but you will help me. I need to find out exactly what happened in London."

How had I conjured up such a complicated dream? What could it mean? I snap my fingers. "Oh, I get it. This is my subconscious sabotaging my plan because I'd rather have a mental breakdown than risk being turned down by Greg. Well, jokes on you, I'm still going to steal his mail and go upstairs to see him. Like you said, all fear does is hold a person back."

"Are you unwell?"

I laugh then stop abruptly. "Probably."

He rubs his chin with one hand. "Have you considered the possibility that I'm here to help you find your confidence?"

Mike wiggles out of my hold and jumps to the floor. I let him go. "Like a guardian angel?"

"Something like that."

"I don't know if I want one. It was bad enough when everything only made me anxious. If I'm delusional, I'll have to start taking medicine and I don't like to take pills for a headache. How about you go away and we both pretend you were never here?"

"I wish that were possible." After a moment, he asks, "Who's Greg?"

I sigh. "Just the most gorgeous . . ." I stop, look Hugh over, and admit, "The second most attractive man I've ever met. He lives upstairs and I've been trying to get him to notice me."

"Dressed like that?"

My head snaps back. "Rude."

"Sorry." He smiles. "My sense of fashion is likely outdated. Has society become afraid of the female form? Because you're concealing all of yours."

Mouth hanging open, I say, "I work from home, and being comfortable is one of the perks."

"So, you *choose* to dress that way?"

My hands go to my hips. "Times have changed, mister. Men no longer tell women what to wear."

There is a twinkle in his eyes when he says, "I'd never limit what a woman could wear, but I might hope she takes my preference under consideration when dressing for me."

"When dressing *for* you? How androcentric."

"I'm not familiar with that word, but if it means I like to see a little leg now and then—guilty as charged. You don't have preferences when it comes to what you like to see men wear?"

"People are allowed to dress however they want."

"I didn't ask what you allowed them to wear, I asked if you had a preference." His grin turns sinfully sexy. "There's a difference. For example, I'd allow you to touch me any-where, but I have a preference when it comes to where I'd like you to focus your attention."

My mouth rounds, and even though my knee-jerk reaction is to be offended, I find that I can't be when he's smiling at me like he's giving me permission to touch him. I shouldn't. I want to. But I can't. I mean, I can, and it might be safe, but I shouldn't.

Right?

He doesn't seem to sense the battle raging in me. "I bet if you wore a dress you'd easily catch Greg's attention. You're not bad looking."

"First, you're horrible at giving compliments. Second, I

don't wear dresses because I feel ridiculous in them."

"Then you've never worn the right one." He smiles again. "Or worn it for the right man."

I fold my arms across my chest, feeling both understood and exposed at the same time. "I wish you were real."

His expression turns serious. "I wish there weren't things that are more important than how I feel about anything."

"What kinds of things are you talking about?"

He ran a hand through my hair. "Let's make a deal. I'll help you get your man if you help me find my friends."

"Your friends?"

"They were with me at an award ceremony in 1945. Something happened to us that night. I need to know what." He motions toward my phone in my pocket. "You understand this time and place. You could teach me about it, then I'll either find my unit or uncover what happened to them."

"But you're not real."

"You might be right about that, but even if I'm not, as long as I help you overcome your fear and catch Greg's eye—does it matter?"

I chew my bottom lip. "How do you feel about breaking into someone's mailbox?"

"At this point, to find out what happened to my friends—there's nothing I wouldn't do."

# Chapter Eight

*Hugh*

*Munich, Germany*
*1942*

FELT INVINCIBLE until this very minute.

I'm on the side of a dirt road, blood gushing from my back, crawling toward a motionless Allen and what's left of Billy. Jack picks me up, tells me I'm already healing and carries me the rest of the way to our friends.

Five successful missions under our belt and we've been getting cocky. The program stopped giving us injections when we began to heal almost instantly. We still felt pain, but not like we had in the beginning.

I should have paid better attention as we made our way through the woods toward a cave where we heard a German scientist was hiding with his family. We were on foot, dressed to blend in, and didn't expect to meet any resistance.

There was an abandoned truck, some randomly placed

barbed wire, and ravines we made our way around. Looking back, I hate that I missed how those objects funneled us toward a landmine.

We were too confident. Billy paid the price. He exploded like a smashed watermelon. Even we don't come back from something like that.

Allen was closest to Billy. There's enough of him still intact that he should survive and regenerate, but he isn't breathing. The hole in his chest is substantial and might have been enough to kill him.

Jack puts me down beside them. I'm on my knees trying to get Allen's heart pumping again, but it's too damaged.

The rest of the men gather around.

"He's gone," Edward says.

I know he is, but I can't stop trying.

Dead doesn't heal. That's reality, but this wasn't necessary. We could have prevented this. I sit back and let out a primal cry.

Ray snaps, "Leave them. We've already given our position away. The target is likely on the move."

Covered with not only my blood, but that of Allen and Billy, I rise to my full height. Between clenched teeth, I growl, "We don't leave anyone behind. That clear?"

Jack comes to stand at my side. "I'll carry them out."

Ray's lips curl back in a snarl. "Do what you want, I'm going after the target."

Despite the disgust rushing through me, I acknowledge

that as necessary as well. "Jack, take them back. We'll fall back closer to the road. Everyone—use your bayonet to test the ground before you move forward. That's probably not the only mine."

Ray and I exchange a look in the darkness. He and I often disagree, but at the end of the day we're on the same team and I'd give my life to save his if it came to that.

He nods once in agreement. "They'll use the road to attempt an escape."

"They won't get away." I wave for the men to follow me. Although technically I'm not the unit leader this time, Billy won't be issuing orders anytime soon.

Fourteen. That's how many of us are left. Out of over fifty men.

What we're doing matters, though, so we'll keep fighting until the very last one of us is gone. And no one will escape us—not today, not ever.

I pause mid-stride. Is this how every soldier thinks or am I losing my humanity?

I'm glad the program faked my death. I wouldn't want my family to know the man I'm becoming.

# Chapter Nine

*Mercedes*

*Providence, Rhode Island*
*2024*

"So . . . what do you want to do now?"

My question lights a spark of interest in his eyes and his gaze drops to my lips. I flush from head to toe and sway toward him. This isn't my first sex dream, but I don't usually see the face of who I'm with and not this detailed.

Or maybe I'm unable to remember them after I wake. How sad to think I might always be experiencing something this intense only to carry no memory of it back with me.

He's going to kiss me again.

The first time surprised me, but I'm ready this time.

He dips his head closer. Closer. I can feel the heat of his breath on my lips. Something is still bothering me, though, and I blurt, "Why aren't you Greg?"

His expression darkens. "The man upstairs?"

"Yeah. I mean, you're hot and everything, but I'm not into military men. You're a German Shepherd guy, when my preference is Golden Retriever. If this is my dream, then shouldn't you be the man I've spent months thinking about?"

"Months, huh?" He runs a hand through his hair and straightens. "Have you considered that this might not be a dream?"

"Well, the alternative is that I've been so lonely lately my mind created an imaginary friend. I don't want that to be true."

"Or I'm real."

"That would mean I somehow didn't notice you enter my apartment. So, instead of just appearing, you walked in—dressed like that and talking as if you're from the past and time-traveled or something. All of which would imply you're the one who's mentally unstable. Instantly, this situation would go from confusing yet sexy to kind of terrifying."

"So, we're sticking with this being a dream?"

I nod slowly. He steps away, and I'm completely devastated.

He doesn't seem much happier.

After a moment, I decide to stop sucking the joy out of what could have been a fun dream. "Hey, do you know what a television is?"

"Yes. Do you have one?" He looks around the room, not

seeming to understand that the fifty-inch plasma screen on the wall is one.

"I do." I walk over to the coffee table and pick up the remote. "Would you like to watch a movie?" I turn the television on.

He comes to stand beside me. "I've only seen one television and it was in a store. People said everyone would have one in the future."

I kick off my shoes and choose one corner of the couch. "Then sit down and we'll watch a movie."

He glances down at his dress shoes then at his jacket. "Do you mind if I make myself comfortable?"

"N-no," I choke out. "I don't mind."

He bends to unlace his shoes, slides them off, and neatly places them beside the coffee table. When his hand goes to the knot on his tie, he says, "Are you okay if I take off a few things?"

Oh, my God. Oh, my God. I swallow hard. "Yes."

He unbuttons his jacket, removes it, and places it on the back of the couch. I can barely breathe. He loosens his tie, then whips it the rest of the way off before rolling it neatly and placing it on the table. I remember a spicy scene I read recently about a man, his tie, and a whole lot of sex. It was that book in particular that finally convinced me I didn't want to die a virgin. When his hand goes to the top button of his shirt, he pauses and meets my gaze as if there's a chance I might protest.

I nod and don't even try to look away.

He unbuttons it halfway down, then pulls his shirt up and out of his trousers and finishes the job, revealing, sadly, yet another layer of clothing: a light brown cotton undershirt. "That's better."

"Yes," I croak. The less he wore the better looking he became. He's muscular, but not in the big and bulky way men who frequent the gym are. No, he's simply head-to-toe toned. Not a single imperfection on him, outside of a white scar around one of his fingers.

After placing his shirt on top of his jacket, he sinks onto the other side of the couch. I lift a blanket off the floor, tuck it around myself, and try to pretend I do this all the time. "What kind of movie would you like to watch?"

"Something set during this time period. I'd like to see how much the world has and hasn't changed."

"Can you stomach a romantic comedy?"

"Is that what you like?"

I shrug. "Sometimes. I don't like to watch anything sad because reality is often sad enough."

"Do you have a favorite?"

"I do." I smile. "But it's an oldie. Not as old as you are. Maybe twenty or so years. It's my comfort movie."

"Then I'd like to see it."

I search for which streaming service offers it, then choose it. "It's corny, but her yearning for a family hits hard every time."

"Because you miss your own?"

I start the movie and sit back, pulling the blanket higher on me. "Because I don't. I always wanted the kind of family that chooses to be together. My parents are good people, but I just kind of happened to them and they stepped up and were responsible, yet as soon as I was old enough to be on my own, they started smiling. I don't resent that—I just wish . . ."

"Come here," he says in a deep voice.

My eyes fly up to meet his.

He raises an arm and waves me over to his side. "If we're going to watch a movie about wishing things were better than they are, I'll need a hug too."

Is he serious?

If this is a dream, I don't have to be me. I can be whoever I want to be. I raise the blanket a little and wink at him. "I think you should come here."

His laugh is deep and warms me to the core. "How about we meet in the middle?"

"I accept those terms." I scoot a little toward him. He moves a little toward me. I offer him part of the blanket and he pulls it over both of us before tucking me against his side.

The movie begins and I give in to an impulse to snuggle closer. His arm tightens around me. "Hugh?"

"Yes?"

"I don't want to wake up from this dream."

He inhales deeply, his chest rising and falling against me.

"Good because I don't think we can."

That declaration should have sounded scary, but it didn't. Wrapped in the cocoon of him, nothing could hurt me.

"She has bad taste in men," he murmurs when Sandra Bullock declares her love for a gorgeous man who had yet to notice her.

"He represents everything she thinks she wants. That's the point. He's employed, well dressed, polite . . ."

He makes a sound deep in his chest.

During the scene in the hospital when the unconscious man's family mistakes her for his fiancée, Hugh shakes his head. "Lying to his whole family? How does anyone come back from that?"

"She didn't mean to," I defend. "The nurse overheard her voicing a wish. All she did was not correct a misunderstanding. Besides, keep watching, that's the least of her problems."

It doesn't take him long to discern the whole plot. "She's got it bad for his brother."

"She does, but that's not why I love this movie."

When the heroine of the movie is celebrating Christmas with the family of her fake fiancé, Hugh tilts his head and looks at me. "That's the kind of family you wish you had?"

I sigh. "Isn't it what everyone wants?"

"I don't know—not anymore. You think lover boy upstairs can give you that?"

"Maybe." I shrug. "There's only one way to find out."

"Steal his mail?"

I elbow his ribs. "It's not technically stealing, since I'm going to give it right back to him."

"You have a complicated moral compass."

"I choose to take that as a compliment."

"It wasn't an insult, merely an observation."

I snuggle closer and stop talking because I don't want to think about anything beyond how good it feels to not be alone. The movie ends and I look for an excuse for us to remain side by side. "Hungry?"

"I am, actually."

I stand and wave a hand at the kitchenette. "I have leftovers from yesterday if you want them."

He follows me to the kitchen. Opening my refrigerator, I inspect the meager contents. *I couldn't have dreamed up some good snacks?* "I wasn't expecting company, so it looks like you can choose between half of a sandwich I bought from a sub shop yesterday or a pickle."

The corner of his mouth curls and his expression softens with humor. "How are you still single?"

The glare I shoot him doesn't lessen his amusement. "You, sir, have outdated expectations of gender roles. Women don't cook anymore."

His grin is so damn sexy I have trouble remembering why I'm annoyed. "I like it when you call me sir."

"Are you even listening to me?"

"I can see I have my work cut out for me. Has flirting also fallen out of fashion?"

My mouth drops open. "Of course it hasn't. And I am very good at flirting—when it's with someone I'm interested in."

"Really? Pretend I'm your upstairs lover boy. What would you say to me right now?"

I laugh-snort, realize how unsexy that is, then roll my shoulders back and meet his gaze. Oh, I'll show him. I lower my eyelids in what I hope is a sultry move and bring my hands to my hips. Sadly, I can't think of a single sexy thing to say.

He comes closer and leans a hip against the counter a mere foot away. "Hey, Doll, did it hurt when you fell from heaven—"

I laugh-snort again. "Sorry, I know I'm the one choosing what you say, but that's too much. I can't accept that, not even from myself."

"That bad, huh?"

I nod and smile.

He moves closer and I back up until I'm pressed against the refrigerator. He places his hand beside my head and leans in. When he speaks, his tone is low and gravelly. "You're the answer to questions I never thought my heart would ask."

His gaze is intense.

The warmth of his breath teases my lips.

"How's that?" he asks just above a whisper.

It takes everything in me to not throw my arms around him and demand that this particular spicy dream ends with me finally knowing what sex is like. The only thing holding me back is the knowledge that I always wake before that part and waking isn't something I'm willing to risk. "That's pretty good," I admit.

He straightens and steps away. "Now you try it."

"Try it?"

"How would you catch my attention?"

I say the first thing that comes to mind. "Trip you?"

His deep laugh rumbles out. "If all modern women are as funny as you are, landing in the future might not be such a bad thing."

Without a word, I open the refrigerator, pull out the half sandwich and toss it to him. The idea of him with someone else shouldn't bother me since soon I'll wake and likely remember none of this. To occupy myself, I retrieve my uneaten plate of chicken from the table and dump the dried contents in the trash before rinsing the plate and putting it on a towel beside the sink.

Seeking an outlet for my growing frustration with myself I look around the floor for what I know must be there. Hugh places the sandwich on the table and asks, "What's wrong?"

"Nothing," I say angrily. "I'm just trying to make sense of this dream, and I don't get it. I don't understand what you're doing here. Why am I torturing myself with you? And where's my favorite fork?"

Hugh takes a step toward me, then stops. Mike sneak attacks his leg from beneath the table. "What the hell?"

Mike jumps up on the table and says something in cat that I can only assume is rude before he turns and wiggles his tail at him. I sweep my cat into my arms. "Sorry, Mike hasn't met many people." Mike lets out a sound in protest, but I don't put him down. "Are dreams our way of working through our fears? If so, I don't know how this is supposed to help. I already know I'm socially lame and my cat has bad manners. When I wake up, won't I feel worse about both?" I look down at Mike. "If I finally get a date with Greg and you attack him—I'm throwing away your catnip." Mike's protest this time involves extending his nails into my arm, which wins him a deposit onto the floor.

Hugh nods toward Mike. "I know what his problem with me is."

I lift and drop my shoulders, glad one of us does.

Hugh continues, "He knows I was the fork."

*Yeah, let that one sink in.*

"You were what?"

"Your favorite fork. I can't explain how or why I was in that silverware, but it's why we don't feel like strangers. I know the taste of you. I've been in your mouth so many times. You've held me, licked me, washed me . . ."

I start to laugh . . . then choke. The temperature in the room soars. "If this is you trying to show me how to flirt again—"

"No, it's the truth. I thought letting you believe this was a dream would help, but it's only confusing you more. This is real. In 1945 I was at an award dinner with my unit. Something happened that night that I thought ended all our lives. But it didn't. It put me in that box, and kept me in some kind of suspended animation until you set me free."

"From being silverware?"

"Yes."

"As my fork?" I sink onto one of the chairs at my kitchen table. There's no way this is real. "Were you part of a government secret super soldier program?"

"I was."

"And you joined it because it was the only way you could serve in World War II?"

"Exactly."

I laugh a little hysterically. "So your origin story is the same as Captain America. God, I'm unoriginal."

"I don't know a Captain America."

"Of course you don't. He's in the Marvel Universe and you—you're in the universe of Mercedes's mental break-down. I was really hoping you were a dream. Oh, my God." I flap my hands. "If I can't get rid of you, I'm going to lose my job, my apartment, and Mike." I bend over, gasping for breath as I hyperventilate. I close my eyes. "Please go away."

"Mercedes."

"No. I'm not doing this. I'm too close to having a nor-mal life for you to come here and mess that up. I'm going to count to ten, and when I open my eyes again you'll be—"

"Still here. Ten. Open your damn eyes, Mercedes. I'm not going anywhere. I need your help."

"*My* help?" I blink a few times quickly, then glare at him. "Look around. I'm barely surviving. What kind of help do you think I could be?"

The way he's looking at me, like I'm important to him, has me all kinds of confused. I would love this to be true. To be needed by a man like him? To be called to do something important for once? I ache from yearning as I meet his gaze.

"Just because you've failed at things in the past, doesn't mean you should give up on making a difference. I've done horrible things in the name of saving the world—things that didn't change the outcome in the end. We didn't stop the atomic bomb from being developed. All that training. All those casualties on both sides—for nothing, but I'm still here, and I have to believe that's not a mistake. I will find out what happened to the rest of my unit and if there's work for us to do here."

I rise to my feet. "I need you to leave."

"I'm not going anywhere."

"If you don't—I'll—I'll call the police."

"And tell them what? You're not even sure I'm real."

Stomping a foot, I rub a hand over my face. "I don't believe in violence, but I could hit you."

"Good."

A growl of frustration bubbles out of me. I don't understand him or how he makes me feel. "Good? That's good?"

"Yes. Maybe if you get angry enough you'll figure out you're not helpless. You're not crazy either. This isn't a dream or a hallucination. This shit is real and I don't have a lot of options right now."

"If I agreed to help you, what would that entail?"

"Just finding answers."

I moved to the city for a fresh start, but so far, I'm ninety-nine percent the person I've always been. One of my favorite TikTok creators posted a meme about the power of saying yes to opportunities and adventures. She said it had completely changed her life.

Could I do the same?

"This could be *my* origin story."

"I don't know what that means, but sure, it can be your story—the one where you solve a puzzle and get the guy."

"The guy?"

"Upstairs Loverboy."

# Chapter Ten

*Hugh*

*Providence, Rhode Island*
*2024*

HER EYES FILL with confusion and hurt.

I'm an ass.

She's attracted to me and damned if I'm not attracted to her too. The temptation to sweep her into my arms and carry her off to her bedroom is strong, but it's a distraction I can't allow. Not yet.

I shouldn't have snuggled with her on the couch. All that achieved was to remind me how long it's been since I was with a woman. The hunger in her eyes has me imagining licking every inch of her until she begs me to be inside her again.

Her gaze lowers to my crotch and my dick swells in anticipation. Does she know what she's doing to me? She claims she's never been with a man and there is an innocence about her.

When she raises her eyes to meet my gaze again, I can see the question she won't voice. She wants to know why, even though I seem interested, I still want her to be with him.

Damn it all to hell.

I went to war to protect the innocent and carry the guilt of not always doing that well. What am I supposed to do with a woman who clearly hasn't been exposed to the darker side of humanity?

"It's not that I don't find you attractive." Her eyes round, and I don't stop because some things need to be said. "I do, but nothing can happen between us. It wouldn't be safe for you."

"Safe?"

My objective is murky even to me. If she were a friend's sister, I'd gently tell her that if the man upstairs hadn't noticed her yet, he didn't deserve her. Why settle for less than someone who lights up when they see you?

But I also don't want her to see me as a viable option. I'm not. Sure, I'm not handling any of this well, but waking up eighty years in the future can mess with a person's head.

"I'm strong. Maybe too strong. All of us were afraid to have sex after our treatments because we didn't want to hurt anyone. We vowed to wait until we knew a woman could survive it."

Her eyes widen even more. "Oh."

"So, although I appreciated the snuggle earlier, I would

never risk your safety."

"That's good." She lets out a shaky, somewhat disappointed breath.

I fight back a smile. *Same, Doll. Same.*

"What did they do to you?" she asks in a soft voice full of concern, and I wonder what might have been had we met under any other circumstance.

During the war, I wouldn't have told her so much as my real name, but the war is over, and so are any promises made to keep the government's secrets. I'm in her home, asking her for help. She deserves the truth.

"I can regrow limbs." I show her my finger and point to the white line on it. "Childhood accident. It was enough to stop me from being eligible for the Army. So, when I was approached by a government program that promised me a way to serve, I jumped at the chance and agreed to everything without any idea of what it might entail."

"So you can't die?"

"I'm not invincible. None of us were. It took a month for my finger to grow back. The more treatments they gave us, the quicker we could heal, but you must be alive to heal. We lost some good men before we understood that."

She swallows visibly and bends to study my finger. "What's the white line?"

"A scar. We all have them. We heal, but never completely from larger injuries." I turn so my back is toward her and lift my shirt. The cool air of her apartment rushes over my exposed skin. "I thought I was dead when this happened to me, but I was healed by the next day." I shuddered beneath the light touch of her hand as she traced the scars on my back.

"Did it hurt?"

"Like a bastard." I lower my shirt and turn back to face her. "And it scared me. I woke up in a full sweat many times afterward and it was always the same—my mind replayed the moment I knew there was no escape. It's funny how time slows down when you think you're going to die."

"That must have been terrifying, but you didn't quit. You kept working for them?"

"I didn't have a choice, but even if I'd been given one, I wanted to be there. We were making a difference. At least, we thought we were."

Her expression softens. "I'm sorry."

"Don't be. Life is like that sometimes." I run a hand down one of her arms, savoring the feel of her. "What we want to happen isn't always possible."

She studies my face. "You feel real."

"Because I am."

Shaking her head, she says, "Okay. Let's do this. Let's find out what happened to your unit."

"How?"

"We'll start with my laptop."

"Your laptop?"

"It's a computer like my phone but much easier to do

searches on. Hang on, I'll go get it."

When she returns, I'm seated on the couch. She inhales visibly, nods, then joins me. I adjust my arm so she can slide closer to me with her laptop. I expect her to type but she puts it on my lap and points to a rectangular box on the screen. "This is just like on my phone. When you type here you're accessing AI enhanced internet. I don't fully understand how the whole thing works, but think of the internet like a huge database of information and AI as something that helps you sort through it. Not everything it'll answer will be true. In fact, it's getting harder and harder to determine what's real online and what isn't—especially with AI-generated videos."

"What is AI?"

"Artificial intelligence." She chews her bottom lip. "Really, really smart computers that have started to think on their own."

"That sounds dangerous."

"Yeah, we're all a little freaked out by it, but it's coming whether or not we want it, so you might as well learn to use it."

"Like the bomb." I shouldn't have said that. After that downer comment, neither of us seems to know what to say.

She wrinkles her nose. "Okay, so, type in a question and let's see what we find."

I think about my last moments in 1945 and the technology I heard was being experimented with. The Philadelphia

Experiment sounded implausible when I heard about it, but I was living proof that things didn't need to sound possible to happen. So I type: **Could a magnetic blast turn someone into silverware?**

The screen changes, and a response appears: **Theoretically, a blast of a magnetic field could cause the atoms or molecules of someone to break their chemical bonds and reform in a new configuration.**

I type: **Is there any evidence of anyone being turned into an inanimate object by a magnetic field weapon?**

The computer answered: **Such a concept is purely fictional and belongs in the realm of works of fantasy or science fiction. The human body is composed of complex biological matter that cannot be reconfigured into metal by any current technology.**

At my side, Mercedes says. "Don't get discouraged. Even AI has limits. It wouldn't have access to government secrets." She taps her chin. "Unless they're unclassified. I know some documents are automatically declassified. Ask where we can find declassified documents."

I do and the computer produces a list: National Archives and Records, CIA Electronic Reading Room, National Security Archive, Library of Congress . . . Some allow online access, which I assume means on computer as well as in-person.

A spark of hope lights in me. Learning how to utilize modern technology might intimidate some people, but I survived nearly being cut in half. I can do this.

We start by searching for my name in connection to

World War II. It takes several tries, but eventually we find a death certificate for me. Cause of death? Fire. Body charred beyond recognition. No record of me enlisting. That all made sense, but shouldn't our names have come out after the war ended?

I search for the men in my unit. They're listed as long dead and each with causes of death that left their bodies so damaged they weren't identified by witnesses and location.

Were they all dead? Or, like me, somehow still alive?

Mercedes shifts against me, and I loop an arm behind her shoulders.

*I will do this.*

*I will figure out what happened to my friends.*

# Chapter Eleven

*Mercedes*

*Providence, Rhode Island*
*2024*

I WAKE SLOWLY without opening my eyes and smile as I relive my favorite parts of a dream I succeeded in holding on to. I never considered myself a particularly creative person, but every single detail is vivid like a memory. If watching superhero movies inspires that kind of dream, I'm never watching anything else.

My blankets are tucked tightly around me, keeping me beautifully warm. I snuggle into them and freeze when one part tightens around me—like an arm. It's only then that I realize the pillow beneath my cheek is muscular with a heartbeat. Yes, I'm beneath a comforter, but I'm not alone.

I inhale deeply and decide heaven smells like cedarwood and cinnamon. *Hugh.*

My eyes fly open and I tip my head back to confirm

what I already know. He's not only still here, but he's wrapped around me. Our legs are intertwined. One of my arms is trapped beneath the weight of him and is numb, but I don't care.

The last thing I remember doing last night was resting my head on his shoulder as he continued typing questions and following links. I'm not sure what it says about the evolution or lack thereof of humanity that it had taken him very little time to get as good at using the internet as I am.

He stirs against me, and for the first time in my life, I feel the nudge of a man's excitement against my hip. Yep, that's what that is.

I've read my share of romances. I know where this could go with very little effort. All I have to do is slide my hand down between us and give him a little encouragement. He'd groan and lose control. I'm not on birth control, but he has eighty-year-old sperm so . . . there's that. If fiction is to be believed at all, kissing Hugh's neck would drive him wild. He'd rip my clothing off, claim every inch of me, then—

Wait, he said sex with him might hurt me. Not the way the hero in a romance tells a virgin he's afraid of her discomfort. No, if anything he said was to be believed this would be a super soldier fucking that no one in his unit was sure a woman could survive.

That doesn't sound like a good choice for my first time.

Maybe I shouldn't touch his dick.

I ease myself off it and slide my arm out from under him.

I'm on my feet when his hand closes around my still-clothed leg.

"Hey."

I smile and hope he can't tell how nervous I am. "Good morning."

"You okay?"

I nod.

"I didn't find anything on Inkwell, but there were places that said some documents could only be seen in person." As he speaks, he runs his hand up and down the back of my thigh. "Would you drive me to those places?"

If he's trying to manipulate me by getting me all hot and bothered for him, it's working. In that moment, I wouldn't refuse him anything. In a strangled voice, I say, "You're pretty handsy for a man who can't put out."

"Sorry." He laughs and drops his hand. "So, would you?"

Put out? I shake my head. No, he's asking about driving him somewhere. He's laying on the charm because he needs my help, but I've never had a man look at me like I'm a temptation he might not be able to resist. It's exhilarating. I clear my throat. "Not with you dressed like that. If we're going anywhere we need to get you some new clothes."

"I don't have any money."

I roll my eyes. "That makes you no different than the last two men who asked me out."

His eyes narrow as he pushes himself to a seated position. A more sophisticated woman might have looked away as his muscles rippled and he stretched, but I don't pretend it isn't a mesmerizing view. "I'm losing confidence in your ability to choose a good man for yourself. I may not approve of Loverboy upstairs. What do you know about him?"

His expression is so serious I start to laugh. There's just something about a fork questioning my dating practices that tickles my sense of humor. Gasping for air and waving at him, I say, "If he's not up to your standards . . . what would you do? Fork him up?"

Hugh groans and stands.

I inhale sharply. Every inch of him is toned and my body comes alive with anticipation. Still, I can't stop from poking at him more. "Thankfully, my social life is none of your forking business."

He steps closer. "Done yet?"

I choke on a giggle. "Not even forking close."

He nods and purses his lips. "You're getting good at this."

"At what?"

"Flirting. And I like it."

"Thank you?"

He nods toward my T-shirt and sweatpants. "I'll let you buy me clothing today."

I roll my eyes again. What a gentleman.

He bends and growls in my ear. "As long as you let me choose clothing for you. I want to see you in a dress." His lips trace down my neck. "And maybe out of it."

It's nearly impossible to breathe when he kisses the line of my jaw. "You said that was dangerous."

Raising his head so his face is above mine, he licks his bottom lip and then flicks his tongue across mine. "Then you should stop looking at me like . . ."

"Like what?" I ask breathlessly.

"Like you want this." His mouth closes over mine. I give myself over to the roughness of the kiss and cling to him, opening my mouth for him. He's demanding, but in no rush. His hands take hold of my arms and he holds me immobile while his tongue slips inside my mouth and intimately dances with mine.

He lifts his head.

I'm glad he's holding my arms so I don't melt at his feet.

We stand there for several minutes, breathing raggedly. The conflict raging within him is clear in his dark eyes. Is my excitement obvious in mine? No one has ever come close to making me feel this way.

"God, I want to—"

"Fork me?" I giggle nervously.

A laugh rumbles out of him and he lays his forehead against mine. "You're growing on me, Mercedes Hopper."

Still giddy from his kiss, I hold his gaze and smile. "You're growing on me too."

There's an intensity to the moment. If I pulled his face back to mine, we wouldn't be going anywhere but to my bed today. I take a deep breath and search for the courage, but before I do, he kisses the end of my nose and steps back; the moment is gone.

"Do you need the bathroom before I shower?"

He shakes his head.

"I'll be quick."

"No rush. I'll search the internet."

Nodding, I open my laptop for him and put in the passcode. "There you go. All set."

I take a fast shower, dress in jeans and a T-shirt, and dig through the bathroom cabinet for makeup but give up when I can't find more than mascara. The woman looking back at me from the mirror doesn't need blush, she's pink and flushed already. I almost tie my hair back in a ponytail, but decide to leave it down for once.

Hugh is hunched over my laptop and typing when I enter the living room again. When he senses I'm here he looks up. His eyes light up in a way that rocks me back onto my heels. He smiles as he stands. "Not bad," he says as he looks me up and down. "You clean up nicely."

"Would you like to shower? I'll show you how it works."

"If water still comes out of a pipe, I'll figure it out."

"It does." I clear my throat. "You can use any of the towels in there."

"Thanks." As he walks past, he gives my ass a slap. "Yep, you look good in denim."

I jump and spin to look at him.

His shoulders shake like he's holding in laughter.

"Modern men keep their hands to themselves," I call after him.

"I'm not a modern man."

A smile spreads across my face.

*He sure isn't.*

# Chapter Twelve

## *Hugh*

*Providence, Rhode Island*
*2024*

THE FUTURE IS surprisingly not that different from my time. Some things have changed: everything has more buttons, makes annoying sounds, and people are hyper-focused on their personal safety. Helmets are a big thing. Not just in a war. Not sure if that means people's heads have gotten softer over time, but the first thing Mercedes tells me when we climb into her car is that I need to restrain myself with a strap across my lap and chest. This supposedly will protect me from bashing my head if her driving lacks finesse.

I remind her I heal quickly.

She says the police will pull us over if I'm not safely restrained. It's the law.

The government has been busy making a lot of laws.

To protect people.

According to Mercedes.

I didn't fight to free the world to agree to be coddled like a child.

I keep those thoughts to myself because Mercedes looks excited about taking me out into the world. She pulls into a garage that reminds me of a military vehicle storage building, but instead of being one floor, it goes up and up and up.

She parks and gives me permission to free myself from the belt. When I meet her behind the car, I take a moment to appreciate how she's braver than she gives herself credit for. She navigated the busy streets without issue. There was more than one man in my unit who never drove a car before the war. Some of them found the initial experience as intimidating as receiving our weekly mystery shots.

I was fortunate enough to drive delivery vehicles for work. As Mercedes and I walk through a set of glass doors, I say, "May I drive your car back?"

She gives me an odd look. "Do you have a license?"

"To drive?"

"Yes, to drive."

"I have identification."

She shakes her head. "You need to pass a driving test and have a license issued by the state before you can legally drive."

"Because it's the law?"

"Yes."

Of course.

Inside the building other people step onto something I heard about but had never been on—an electric stairway. Mercedes steps forward with confidence, so I follow her lead.

"So, this is the Providence Place Mall."

"It's big." Bigger than anything we had in my town, but cities like New York might have had a building this size. Europe hadn't. At least, not where we were. We stepped off the electric stairs and I paused to take in the sheer size of the interior of the building. The center was open to the floors below. In all directions, storefronts lined the walls. Everything was bright, shiny, and . . . flashier than I was used to.

Couples walk by with children, looking as they always had, except both are dressed in denim or slacks, and no one greets anyone as they pass. The future is a busy place, but determining what everyone is rushing around for is difficult.

"I think I know what you'll look good in, if you trust me," Mercedes says tentatively.

My attention returns to her. "I'm sure I'll like whatever you suggest."

Together we walk down a hallway. I pause at the storefront full of women's underclothing fully on display for all to see. Mercedes doesn't appear to notice it. I'm glad I've always had a good poker face.

She stops in front of a shop. "This seems like your style." J. Crew. It did indeed appear to have clothing I would be comfortable in.

As soon as we enter the store a young man comes over

and whistles at me. "Now that's charisma. Is that an OC?" I don't understand and it must show because he adds, "Is it an original character?"

I look to Mercedes for assistance.

She's beaming. "You can see him?"

The young man laughs. "Good one. And I get it. I have my own sense of style and I don't give out my trade secrets because I don't want anyone copying me either."

I nod without speaking.

Mercedes grips my arm and shakes it with glee. She beams a smile at me. "He can *see* you."

I tuck her to my side and keep my voice low. "We should probably keep our joy about that to ourselves."

"Of course," she says without letting go of my arm and turns to the young man. "I'd like to buy a couple modern outfits for my very real friend. Could you help us find a few things that would fit him?"

"Sure," the young man answers. "Let me set you up with a changing room."

A quick glance around confirms women's clothing is also available. "Could you also bring a few dresses for her? Something you think would catch a man's eye."

The young man winks at me. "Gotcha. I'll put the two of you side by side. Wish you could share a room, but my boss is here today and she's a prude."

"I'm glad I shaved my legs," Mercedes murmurs and I gurgle on a laugh I'm sure she wouldn't appreciate. I'm a man in my prime with a good amount of appreciation for the opposite sex. Mercedes has me lusting about her one moment then nearly cooing that she's so adorable the next. I don't know what to do with the feelings she's stirring in me.

Mercedes goes into the small room the young man leads us to. I stand outside the one he says I can use. From the doorway of her changing room, Mercedes whispers, "This is kind of fun."

I smile. "It is."

I can't remember the last time I felt young and carefree, but shopping with Mercedes is a treat. The young man fills my room with clothing for me to try on then returns with a stack of dresses for Mercedes.

She and I exchange one last look before closing our doors. I'm impressed by the selection provided. Denim, a gray and black striped sweater, as well as a dark gray wool topcoat. Not bad. It all fits too. I step out of the room and knock on her door. "I'll show you mine if you show me yours."

She laughs. "Okay, but prepare yourself—it's pink."

I suck in a breath when she pokes a head out tentatively, then comes to stand before me in the sweetest linen, knee-high dress and white sweater. "It reminds me of cotton candy."

"Right? It's that bad."

"No." I brush some of her hair back from her eyes and cup her head. "It's that good. I could eat you up in that."

Her mouth rounds. "So, yes?"

"Yes."

Her eyes slowly, oh, so slowly, make their way down the length of me. "You look good too."

"So this is a keeper?"

"Oh, yeah."

I run my fingertips over her parted lips. "I'll pay you back as soon as I can. My priority is my unit, but I won't forget your kindness."

Her breath warms my thumb and I fight the urge to drag her into that room and show her how much I want her. I can't, though. I need to stay focused on finding out what happened to the others. Sex has never been a good enough excuse to leave a war buddy behind.

"I'm just so glad you're real," she gushes.

I shake my head, acknowledging to myself that it would be easier for both of us if I weren't. "Go try on another dress."

Over the next half hour, I approve of every damn dress she models for me and realize it might be her that's impossible not to find attractive. With each outfit and compliment I give her, she gets bolder until she's spinning in the dresses before me, and I'm struggling to remember why this can't be my life.

For me, I decide on a pair of denim as well as a more formal pair of pants, a few shirts, and that wool blazer. With her encouragement, I also choose the most comfortable pair of sports footwear as well as dress shoes. Both are a world better than anything the government ever issued me.

We're both hungry after shopping. So, dressed in our new clothing, we put the bags in her car. She offers to take me to dinner. Having seen the contents of her refrigerator, I suggest we stop at a grocery store instead. "I'll cook for you," I promise. It's the least I can do, considering she bought clothing for me. Not having my own money stings my pride a little, but I'm someone who never says something I don't mean. Soon enough, I'll repay Mercedes tenfold.

Nothing in my life has prepared me for how large grocery stores have become. Like the shopping mall, the place where people buy food is now even called super and I have to agree. Aisles and aisles of more types of food than a person could ever know how to choose from and much of it from all corners of the world.

Mercedes is pushing a shopping cart when she suddenly turns to me and says, "What do you like?"

I shrug. "Meat. Potatoes. Vegetables."

"Come on. There must be something you're craving."

Outside of her? "Anything with sugar. We didn't get much of that."

Her face lights up. "I'm not good at cooking many things, but I love to bake. How do you feel about chocolate?"

"Love it."

"Brownies?"

"What are those?"

"Like cake but flatter and in squares."

"Fudge squares?"

"Maybe. I'll make some for you and you tell me."

"Deal."

She stops and searches my face. "Were you joking about being my favorite fork?"

"No."

She chews her bottom lip. "Do you really think your friends might be stuck in the other silverware?"

I raise and lower a shoulder. "I'm hoping they are because then there's a chance they're not dead and I can save them."

She reaches down, picks up a box, and waves it at me. "We should use plastic utensils until we know for sure."

# Chapter Thirteen

*Mercedes*

*Providence, Rhode Island*
*2024*

I F HUGH IS upset that we didn't find out anything new from our trip to the Providence Library, he doesn't mention it. Laden with bags of food and clothing, we walk into my building just as a female postal worker enters the hallway.

I exchange a look with Hugh. We talked about getting Greg's mail, but that was before I slept in Hugh's arms and spent the day laughing with him. I want to tell him I changed my mind, but he misreads the way I keep looking from him to the postal worker.

He approaches her and lays on the charm. "Got anything for apartment 414?"

She flutters her lashes at him and preens. "That you?"

He winks. "Sure is."

"Well, then I'll see what I have for you."

I make a gagging sound that neither of them acknowledges.

She coyly holds out a few pieces of mail toward him. "Here you go."

He accepts it with a pleased smirk that makes me want to kick him in the shin. "Have a great day."

"Oh, I will," she answers.

Once we're in the elevator and alone, I mimic him and his smile. "Have a great day."

He frowns. "You wanted his mail, I got you his mail."

My mouth snaps shut, and I look around. The earlier easygoing Hugh is gone. His shoulders are tense, and his jaw is clenched. Should I tell him I don't really want the mail anymore?

The elevator opens to my floor and I stumble when I see Greg at my door. He smiles and waves. "Hey. Good timing. I was just coming by to see if you have my mail."

The growl Hugh makes beneath his breath confuses me. He shifts one of the bags he's holding and waves the mail in his hand toward me. "It's right here."

I take it from him because he looks about to shove it into my hand. "Right here."

"Awesome. Those bags look heavy," Greg says. "Let me take one."

He lifts one of the bags out of my arms. Then accepts the mail. "And you just had it on you. That's convenient."

I didn't have much of a choice. I had to play along. "I was going to drop it by earlier then forgot and it made it to my car. I was going to put the food away and walk it up-stairs."

"Glad I saved you a trip." Greg follows Hugh and me to the door of my apartment. "We haven't met," he says to Hugh, "but I heard there was a man living with Mercedes. Nice to finally meet you. I'm Greg."

*He'd heard there was a man living with me? Oh, Mike.* "Mike," I say quickly to Hugh as I open the door, hoping Hugh remembers the cover story for my cat.

Hugh makes a sound I'm not sure how to interpret.

Greg looks from Hugh to me and back. "Are the two of you . . ."

"If you're asking if she's single, she is," Hugh says in an indifferent tone that cuts through me. "Completely single."

Greg's mouth opens then shuts as if he was about to say something then changed his mind. The interest that sparks in his eyes should have moved me, but it doesn't.

I retrieve the bag from Greg, thank him, and close the door in his face. "Hugh."

His back to me, Hugh drops the other bags on the table. His shoulders are bunched with tension, and I don't under-stand why.

He spins on his heel and starts toward the door. "I'm going out. I need some fresh air."

I rush to block his exit. "Wait. Don't go."

"Mercedes, step aside. All I need is a walk. I'll be back."

The feelings bubbling in me are too intense to express. I want to reassure him Greg ceased to matter the moment we met, but Hugh clearly announced he and I are not together. One good day together didn't make a relationship. Still, there is no denying his mood shifted after seeing Greg.

Could he be jealous?

Is that even something you can ask a man? I don't have the nerve to. Instead, I say, "Thank you for getting the mail for me."

He nods without meeting my gaze.

"Are you upset I didn't tell Greg your real name?" I ask.

He shakes his head. "No. And I'm not upset."

"Please don't—"

He picks me up as if I weigh nothing and gently places me out of his way. My mind scrambles as I imagine being with someone that strong, but before I say anything he's gone.

# Chapter Fourteen

## *Hugh*

*Providence, Rhode Island*
*2024*

I'M SEVERAL BLOCKS from Mercedes' house before I slow my pace and address the reason I bolted. Watching Mercedes fawn over Greg hit hard on many levels.

It's not as if she didn't tell me about him. I have no right to feel jealous since she and I are nothing to each other.

*Nothing to each other.* That one stuck with me.

Technically, since everyone I knew is dead, my existence doesn't matter to anyone. I don't matter.

I'm not the soldier who should have been revived . . . brought back . . . woken? Edward was always smarter than I was. He would have already figured out what happened to us by now. He wouldn't still be wondering if any of the unit is also in that silverware.

Me?

Am I saving anyone? No, I'm playing dress-up and matchmaker while falling for a woman who, until we went shopping, was certain I was a figment of her imagination. Sadly, I'm real. *Really* mentally messed up. *Really* out of place in this time period.

I stop in front of the glass window of a bar. A beer or five would take the edge off my mood, but that would require money that, oh, wait, I don't fucking have.

I hate that Mercedes spent money on me instead of the other way around. I need to head back to my childhood home to see if my sister did what I'd asked her to.

A woman walks out of the bar, followed closely by a man. "Leave me alone," she says loudly. "I'm not interested."

"Hey," he slurs the word. "You don't mean that. Come on. You were interested enough to say yes to a drink. At least give me your number."

"No." Her voice rises an octave. She looks around and meets my gaze.

*Understood.*

The man grabs her arm.

I close the distance between us. "She said no."

"Mind your own business," he snarls, maintaining his grip on her.

Two more men, both taller and more muscled than I am, join us. "You okay, Leo?" one asks.

The other one nods to me. "Get out of here."

I look the three men over as I rub my chin. There's a

chance I no longer have enhanced strength or the ability to heal. Does it matter? I glance at the woman, decide it doesn't, and crack my knuckles. I would have stepped in and taken these men on before the war ever started. Sometimes a man has to stand up and protect those around him, regardless of what it costs him. "You heard the lady; she wants to be left alone."

The two blockheads look me over then laugh as if giving someone a beatdown is the entertainment they were hoping for that evening. "I'd run now if I were you," the taller of the two jeers.

I pinch the bridge of my nose. Combat training isn't for the meek. With or without enhanced strength, I learned how to kill a man with one strike. I could neutralize them permanently, but I don't want to. I've seen enough death and war.

The shorter of the two men takes a swing at me. I catch his fist easily and spin his arm until I hear the satisfying sound of bone cracking. He screams, clutching his now limp appendage.

The corner of my mouth curls. My time as a fork hasn't diminished my abilities.

Another man lunges toward me. I grab his shoulder and shatter it as easily as a person could crunch a saltine in their hand. He drops to the ground, swearing. I hadn't meant to be quite so brutal, but I hope they remember this moment the next time they think about disrespecting a woman.

When I turn my attention back to the drunk man, he

immediately releases the woman's arm. "You won't get away with this," he says desperately. "We'll sue you."

I cock an eyebrow at him. "Are you threatening me?"

He pisses his pants right then and there.

"I didn't think so." I nod toward his friends who are each holding their injured parts and moaning. "If I were you, I'd forget about me and get your friends medical attention."

The woman says, "If you even think about suing anyone, I'll press charges for assault. I'll also tell a very different story if asked what happened here. Your friends hurt each other."

The drunk man looks around. "There have to be cameras."

"I hope so, then we can show the world that you're a creep." She's not backing down this time.

He mutters something under his breath then convinces his broken friends to leave with him.

Once we're alone, the woman looks me up and down, her eyes wide with appreciation and heat. "That was amazing."

"Not really, but thanks. Are you okay?"

"Yes, but I wouldn't have been if not for you," she says breathlessly and touches my arm. It's been a long time since I was with a woman and she's pretty, but I'm not interested.

"Happy to have been of assistance."

She steps closer. "*You* could have my number."

With a shake of my head, I say, "Already taken." It isn't a lie. Mercedes is all I crave.

She graciously smiles at my refusal. "All the good ones are. Thank you again."

"You're welcome." I fold my arms across my chest. "Do you have a ride?"

"I just called for one." She looks at her phone. "It's almost here."

"I'll wait until you're safely in it."

And I do.

My mood lifts. I might not have any of the answers when it comes to my situation, but at least I did something good.

I turn on my heel and start to walk away when a male voice calls out. "Hey."

*Are they back for more?*

No, it's not the men from before. The man who jogs up to me is dressed in a conservative, dark suit. His hair is trimmed neatly. "Yes?"

He slows to a stop when he reaches me. "What did you do to those two men?"

"Nothing you need to concern yourself with," I say dismissively.

"You have any fighting experience?"

"You could say that." Humor leaks into my tone.

He leans closer. "You interested in making some fast money tonight?"

Now he has my attention. It'd be nice to repay Mercedes for the clothing and food. "Maybe."

"My boss runs a fight club. You know what that is?"

I don't, but the definition sounds like it's in the name. "Sure."

"There's a fight scheduled in an hour and I was tasked to bring in new talent. Win or lose, you'll get paid if you stay in long enough to give the crowd a show."

"What kind of fighting is it?"

"Two men go into a cage. One man walks out. No weapons, but after that, anything goes. Knock out or to the death. We don't care. The perk of working with us is we'll handle any mess."

"How much could I make?"

"Depends on how many fights you win."

"Assuming I take them all?"

He laughs at what he considers cockiness in my question. "In that case, enough to buy yourself a new car."

Not bad. If I pulled my punches and let my opponents get some hits in, I could draw the fights out. "I'm in."


A FEW HOURS later, I walk to the back office of a warehouse to receive my payout. The man who'd arranged for me to participate in the matches opens a cube-shaped safe and removes a stack of money before closing it again.

He frowns as he hands the cash to me. My knuckles are covered with dried blood, but the wounds beneath have already healed.

I count the bills and groan. It's only a fraction of what we'd agreed to. "Seems like you're a bit short there, chum."

He puts one hand on his waist, pushing his suit coat back and revealing a gun. "Don't worry, we take good care of our own and my boss likes you."

I flex my hands at my side. Eighty years and people aren't any smarter. I'm tired, though, and not looking for another fight. "Pay me what you owe me, and I'll be on my way."

"You're not going anywhere. You work for us now."

I shake my head slowly. "I don't work for anyone. I'll give you one final chance to pay me before I break a few of your bones and just take the money."

He grunts like I made a joke that he didn't find funny, then calls out an order and two men appear at the door.

I roll my eyes skyward. "In my day people like you followed a certain code of conduct. It doesn't have to be like this."

The man nods for his men to step into the room. I tilt my head and crack my neck. *Well, let's go then . . .*

I pocket my money then give the man in charge a look that has him reaching for his gun. That's my cue. I lunge forward and strike sideways with such force that his forearm snaps. I spin and deliver a kick to his other arm, shattering that one as well. One final sweep of my legs and his legs fold sideways as he hits the floor. A man's ability to shoot quickly diminishes once he loses control of his arms. I didn't have to break his legs as well, but he really ticked me off.

The other two fools make the mistake of also drawing

their weapons. Enhanced strength comes with the perk of speed. Distance is my enemy because I'm not impenetrable. I rush forward, grab the gun from one while spinning his arm in my bone-cracking signature move. His scream surprises the other man, giving me an opening. I deliver an upward kick hard enough that he flies up and backward, sliding down the wall, his gun falling to his feet. Three more men fill the doorway and rush me. I take them out as easily. The mistake each new wave of men makes is thinking they can do what the ones before clearly failed at. The floor is covered with unarmed men, some conscious, some unconscious, some swearing, some moaning.

I walk to the safe and twist the hand of it off. When it doesn't immediately open, I pick it up and bend the safe until the locking mechanism releases. Despite the amount of money inside, I count out what I'm owed and take only that.

As I turn to leave, an older man in an expensive suit fills the doorway. He takes in the carnage with fascination rather than fear. "Holy shit. You're going to make me rich."

I pocket my cash. "I wouldn't count on that."

His smile is thin. "I'm going to make you an offer you can't refuse."

"No such offer exists."

"Don't let anger cloud your thinking."

I blink and scratch my head. He's not making any sense. "I'm not angry, but I am leaving."

He looks past me to the mangled safe. "What *are* you?"

"Disappointed."

When I take a step to leave, he says, "You're not going anywhere."

His lack of concern tells me he thinks he has the upper hand. He's not alone. Luckily I am well trained in psychological warfare.

"That's cute that you believe that." I laugh and glance around, then step closer to him. "Before you even think of trying to stop me, ask yourself—do you really believe I don't already work for someone? Or that I'm the only one capable of this?"

"So, what, you're a cop?"

I laugh again. "The people I work for don't believe in governments or laws." I'm nose to nose with him. "I'm leaving. The question you should ask yourself is what story you should tell your people about what happened today. Because if I hear you're out there talking about me, I'm coming back, and not alone. Don't bother to tell your wife and children goodbye, because we'll wipe them out right along with you."

He swallows visibly and pales. "Don't threaten me."

I shrug. "Stay in your lane and I'm no threat to you. Clean this up, forget I was here, and we don't have a problem." I put my hand on his chest and push him back so I can walk past him. "Or die wishing you'd made better decisions. Your choice."

He raises his hand and not one of the five men behind

him make a move as I walk past. If I did have to come for him, his family would be safe, but it's better if I leave him believing that wouldn't be the case.

He'll come up with a story for his men that makes him look smart to have let me go. We've come to an understanding. I doubt he'll be an issue moving forward. Dirtbags like this guy want to be the biggest fish in a small pond.

As I head back to Mercedes's, I'm conflicted. There was a time when I was the good guy.

At least I thought I was.

Now I don't know what the hell I am.

# Chapter Fifteen

## *Mercedes*

*Providence, Rhode Island*
*2024*

A LONE IN MY apartment, I sit across the table from an
irritated-looking Mike. It's as if he knows I lent his
name to Hugh. "I'm not good under pressure," I say in
defense.

Mike's response is to sit back, spread his legs and begin
cleaning where his balls used to be. It's rude and something
that shouldn't be done on the table, but I get it. "I realize
Greg is probably the saner choice, but he doesn't make me
feel the way Hugh does."

Mike meows at me.

I sigh and rest my chin on my hand. "I didn't actually see
Hugh change from a utensil into a man. Did you?"

Mike resumes cleaning himself. I doubt he'd tell me even
if he had.

"People can see Hugh, even Greg could, so he's not a figment of my imagination. If I were sleeping, I think I would have woken up by now. So, either Hugh's a liar who wandered into my apartment and stayed, or this is one of those supernatural events you hear about but never believe could happen to you."

When Mike doesn't show any reaction to either of those possibilities, I say, "Let's worst-case scenario this. I could find out he has a mental condition and an obsession with silverware. Everyone has issues. Greg probably cuts his toenails in the living room like an animal. The point is, I'm not perfect. Not even close. So, it wouldn't be fair for me to expect perfection from someone else, right? And maybe it would be wonderful to be with someone I didn't feel like I have to hide my weirdness from."

I glance down at myself and the pink linen dress I wouldn't have previously imagined feeling pretty in. "I'm not changing *for* him. People should stay true to who they are. But, let's face it, I wasn't even trying to look good anymore."

I sigh.

"I used to like to dress up. I also used to have friends. I don't know what happened to me. The world closed down, and I became comfortable with my life being smaller." I meet Mike's gaze. "But it's not what I want. Don't you see? I came here to shake myself out of that funk. I want to be more than I am—to experience more. Today was magical and Hugh and I didn't really do anything. I like Hugh, and I like who I am when I'm with him."

Mike comes to sit in front of me, tail flicking back and forth.

"You don't have to remind me that it's too early to know. I'm not saying I can imagine spending the rest of my life with him. But like he said, I'm single. Very, very single. Women my age have already had multiple sex partners." I don't know that for sure, but thinking it bolsters my argument. "So, if I want to have sex with a man who believes he served in World War II before he was accidentally transformed into a fork, I'm going to."

*I'm going to have sex.*

*With Hugh.*

I stand and fan my face with a hand.

*What if he says no?*

*Oh, my God, I don't have any sex supplies.*

My stomach lurches but I refuse to let myself negative-think this into not happening. *He cuddles with me. He slaps my ass. A man doesn't do that to a woman he's not attracted to.*

*Right?*

*I'll need condoms.*

*And candles.*

*Wine?*

*Do I have wine glasses?*

Mike silently meows at me and then looks at the cabinet where his food is. I give his head a pat. "You're right, I should also cook something. People say that's the way to a man's heart."

Another silent meow.

"You'll have to find another room to be in. I can't have you looming over us while I lose my virginity."

Mike twirls in front of me impatiently.

"Hugh said he was afraid to hurt me because he's so strong. But he didn't hurt me when he picked me up. He was firm but gentle. And do we really believe he's a super soldier?" When Mike doesn't have an answer for that, I add, "I'm sure that most women, if given the chance, would fork him, and he's super strong." I laugh snort at my own joke. "Fork him. Get it?"

Mike hops down from the table and walks away.

I'm not offended. There's too much to do to worry about why Mike is unhappy with me this time. I set the table with my nicest plates and plastic utensils then use an app on my phone to help choose the best quick meal to make with the ingredients we bought at the supermarket.

On impulse, I set out two wine glasses.

After prepping steaks and some vegetables, I decide to make a quick run to the pharmacy. As I grab my purse, Mike jumps back on the table but I shoo him off. He protests loudly.

"You're right, if I'm doing this, I should do it right. I need lingerie. If Hugh gets back before me, Mike, don't tell him where I went."

Mike stomps away again and I hug my arms around myself. That cat has become my whole world. I do tell him more than he wants to hear, and I know he probably doesn't understand what I'm saying, but he's all I have.

Had.

If I do this right, I'll be able to say I have Hugh as well.

Things are already changing and that's a good thing.

There's a knock on my door. My heart accelerates wildly. Hugh? Already? I'm not ready, but at the same time, I am.

I throw the door open.

*Greg.*

His lopsided, friendly smile that I once fawned over, does nothing for me. I hold the door in one hand. "Yes?"

"I wanted to give you something as a thank-you for making sure my mail got to me." He holds out small bouquet of carnations.

I accept them only because I don't want to be rude. Plus, technically, I stole his mail. "Thank you. You didn't have to, but this is nice."

Since I can't take them with me, I walk back into my apartment with them. He follows me. My father often bought my mother flowers. I don't have a vase because no one, not even me, buys *me* flowers, but I place them beside the sink. Even though I wish the flowers were from Hugh, I'm not going to throw them in the trash.

From a few feet away, Greg says, "Wow, that looks old. What's in it?" He opens the top of the Inkwell box. "Silverware? Cool. Looks like real silver, is it?"

"Don't touch that!" I'm at his side in a heartbeat, closing the box. "Sorry, thank you for the flowers, but I was heading out."

"Oh, of course, sorry. I just love antique things."

"Me too," I say absently as I guide him toward the door and grab my purse. "Thank you again for the flowers."

Just outside my apartment, he gives me an odd look. "I hope I didn't make you uncomfortable. It's obvious I read the situation wrong. I'm not good at meeting new people, and I thought you were trying to ask me out in the elevator the other day. I knew you lived with someone so I didn't want to get involved. I thought when Mike said you were single . . ."

"It's okay," I say in a rush.

He smiles kindly. "I'm so awkward, but I hope we can all be friends after this. You both seem like very nice people."

"Thanks for the flowers. I'll tell Mike they were for both of us."

Greg ducks his head in amusement. "Don't get my ass kicked."

I smile. "I'll try not to."

We separate at the elevator. As I step out of it, I'm feeling lighter—more confident. I spot a woman my age who's retrieving her mail from her box and stop. We've walked by each other countless times since I moved in, even ridden in the elevator together, but I've never said a word to her.

Today, when she glances over her shoulder at me, I smile

and approach. "Hi. I'm Mercedes from the second floor."

"I'm Dazaray," she says. "Third floor."

I'm not afraid. I'm not afraid. "If you'd ever like to get coffee or go for a jog, knock on my door. I'm apartment 227."

Her expression is open and friendly. "I'd love that. Thank you. I hate to jog alone in the city and I'd love the company."

"Great," I say. "Anytime." I back away and head out the front door of the apartment building, kicking myself mentally.

Why did I have to say I jog?

Why couldn't I have come up with something simple like I have your mail?

# Chapter Sixteen

*Hugh*

*Providence, Rhode Island*
*2024*

THE DOOR OF Mercedes's apartment is unlocked when I return. Outside of the blood, there's no sign of cuts or bruises on me from earlier.

I call out to Mercedes, but she doesn't answer. A quick search of the apartment confirms she's not there. The dining room table is set for two—with wine glasses. For me? Mercedes has been nothing but kind to me and how have I repaid her? At the first sign of Loverboy, I'd acted like a jealous schoolboy and stormed off.

Ridiculous.

My only excuse, if I even allow myself one, is that my entire life is upside down and my feelings for her are the only thing that makes sense. I can't imagine a worse way or time to meet someone, but that doesn't change how excited I am to see her again.

I remember teasing Allen for carrying around a photo of a woman who'd broken up with him when he was turned down by the Army. Why he'd fixate on someone who didn't consider him good enough was beyond me, but he said she inspired him. He also said my opinion didn't matter because the heart wants what the heart wants.

That didn't make sense to me until I met Mercedes.

Looking for a hint of where Mercedes might have gone, I enter the kitchen and freeze when I see a bouquet of flowers laid out beside the sink.

A bouquet?

Did she buy flowers for me as well? I pick it up. There's a small card with it with a name and number on it.

Greg's.

I curse. I shouldn't have told Greg that Mercedes is single. That was the green light he was waiting for.

The little fucker didn't waste any time.

I open the refrigerator and scan the contents. Steak and vegetables were prepped on plates, ready to be cooked. I slam the door.

For me or for Greg?

Is she with him now?

A scenario plays out in my head and my temper rises as it does. I imagine her puttering around the kitchen, thinking about me, until Greg shows up with that bouquet. Then what?

Did he kiss her?

Did he carry her up to his place?

Is he fucking her right now?

I shouldn't care. She's not mine.

But I want her to be.

Fuck.

I slam a fist on the countertop. The wooden box of silverware rattles and my mood sinks lower. During the war, even before the award ceremony, I'd felt like I was making a difference—like my life mattered.

Did it?

I reach into the pocket of my jacket, withdraw the wad of cash I won from the club fights, and toss it on the counter next to the wooden box. Being able to repay Mercedes for her kindness feels like a win, but it might have cost me everything.

*Would she have gone with him if I'd stayed when she'd asked me to . . .?*

I lift the cover of the wooden box and take in the neat rows of silverware. Are my friends in there? If so, someone made a mistake when they put me in charge of saving them.

I haven't discovered a fucking useful thing about what happened to us.

My thoughts return to the award ceremony. Images of all of us laughing and joking right before we realized everyone, including the servers, had left. That shouldn't have been enough to concern us, but somehow, we'd known.

There had to have been another sign.

Something we saw.

Something I can't remember.

I shut the cover, but the action doesn't stop memories from tormenting me. In the beginning, we questioned the orders we were given—debated the ethics of some of them. Over time and with each mission we completed, we questioned less. We were on the right side of history and everything we did was for the good of humanity.

But was it?

We handed whole families over to our government, confident it was the only way to prevent a weapon unlike the world had ever seen from being completed. Compassion left us until we acted without kindness or guilt—just a tool wielded by those who went on to use those scientists to do the very thing they'd told us we were preventing.

We didn't save the world.

We didn't save any of the scientists who begged us to free them.

If my friends are indeed trapped in that silverware, maybe they deserve to be.

Maybe I do as well.

Mercedes's cat rubs himself against the side of one of my legs. He turns and flicks his tail at me. Does he know what I did?

I grunt laugh.

Have I now sunk to the level where I'm worried about

what a cat thinks of me?

I've lost my mind.

Glancing back at the box of silverware, I shake my head slowly. *I hope none of you are hoping I'll save you.*

*Nothing we did mattered.*

*We failed ourselves and humanity.*

*I thought I was a hero, but, in reality, I was most useful as a fork.*

That last thought echoes through me as everything goes dark and cold again. I am no one and nowhere, but this time I go there certain I deserve it.

# Chapter Seventeen

## *Mercedes*

*Providence, Rhode Island*
*2024*

SHIFTING BAGS FROM one arm to another to unlock my apartment door, I roll my eyes as I realize it's unlocked. I could blame Greg for distracting me, but I was already distracted by my plans for the evening.

Hugh and his response when I tell him I think we should have sex is all I'm able to think about. *He has to say yes.*

As I close the door behind me, I groan. *I need to calm down.* It's impossible to, though. I know I shouldn't have told the young man who cashed me out at the pharmacy the reason I purchased so many different types of condoms was because I didn't know which kind Hugh would like, but it had spilled out. And when the man's eyebrows rose to his hairline, I shouldn't have asked him if I should purchase anything else, considering it was my first time.

He looked around like he expected someone to be filming our exchange.

Can't really blame him. It's probably not every day a twenty-something-year-old virgin walks in and asks for contraceptive advice. I attempted to clarify my question by bringing up spermicide, but when he went bright red and started coughing, I decided condoms alone would have to be enough for now.

"Hugh?" I call out.

No answer.

That's okay. I'm glad he's not back yet because that gives me more time to prepare. I walk to my bedroom and set the boxes of condoms at the bottom of the bed. Too much?

I move them to the end table beside my bed. After stacking them, I decide the mountain of condom boxes might be intimidating. I don't want to imply that I want to have sex with him a hundred times tonight.

Once.

Maybe twice.

I should put some of the boxes away.

But which ones?

If I leave out the extra-large, will he take that as a compliment or pressure to produce an appendage large enough to fill it?

Would it be better to leave the normal size out and if he can't fit into them use that opportunity to produce an alternative?

*I don't know why I bought the glow in the dark ones.* I stash those in the drawer beside my bed along with the ribbed and flavored ones. I leave the large and normal sized ones out but place them each on different end tables so they wouldn't be the first thing he sees when he enters . . . no, *carries* me into the room.

I take an everything shower, removing hair from all the places I've heard men appreciate smooth surfaces. I shave, pluck, scrub, moisturize, and floss. Standing naked in front of my bathroom mirror, I blow dry and tease my hair to a wild and hopefully sexy height, then change my mind and brush it out into a more sensible style.

I watch a few tutorials on TikTok, then apply my new makeup. It's not every day a woman loses her virginity. I intend to look good while doing it.

Deciding what to wear wasn't difficult after I remembered how Hugh's eyes widened in front of the lingerie store. Now, the workers there had been helpful when I told them my plans.

Sweet wouldn't cut it if I didn't want room for misunderstanding. After stepping into the little black lace teddy that came with a matching garter belt and stockings, I smile at how unexpectedly sexy I look.

Damn.

I won't even have to tell him what I want.

And there's no way, not even a worst-case scenario, in which he could see me like this and refuse.

I grab the candles and place them on the kitchen table. When Mike walks by, I scoop him up and close him into the bathroom with his litter box. He's not happy, but it's for the best.

Feeling uncharacteristically sexy, I go to the kitchen in only the lingerie and start dinner. Only after I've turned on the stove and placed the steaks on a pan in the oven do I notice a pile of money on the counter. A few thousand dollars. Hugh had promised to repay me for the food and clothing. Had he gone to the bank and withdrawn this to do that?

Touched, I bring my hand to my heart. *That's where he must have gone. He should have told me.*

*I thought he was upset with me, but really, he just wanted to repay me.*

I shake my head. *I wonder why he didn't pay for it himself, then.*

*Because having a bank account doesn't fit into his fantasy of being from the past?*

As I place the vegetables in the oven, I talk myself in circles regarding what I'm hoping for.

Repaying me might force him to admit the whole story about him serving in World War II is a lie. I don't want to be with a liar. However, considering I told Greg I had his mail when I didn't, I probably shouldn't judge.

At least I know Hugh isn't a moocher.

When he comes back, I'll tell him I like a man with a

good imagination. People say role-playing keeps things interesting, and I'm willing to find out if that's true.

If he knows I accept him as he is, maybe he'll trust me with the truth about him.

Maybe, like me, he just wants to be more than he is.

I'm a little chilled by the time the steak is done so I wrap a robe around myself. It'll be easy enough to take off when he gets back.

Disappointment begins to kick in when enough time passes that the meal is cold and the surprise of making him dinner promises to be more of a "Surprise, here's what would have been a nice meal."

Still, he'll know I cared enough to cook for him and that's what matters most.

Eventually, I put the food in the refrigerator and go to the couch to wait for him. After a while, I wrap myself in a blanket and decide it's okay to close my eyes for a moment, confident I'll wake when he returns.

# Chapter Eighteen

## *Mercedes*

*Two months later*

I'M STILL TYING the laces on my running shoes when Dazaray knocks on my door and walks in. "Ready?"

"Almost."

Mike twirls around her legs as she walks, prompting her to pick him up for a snuggle. "You sure you're up for adding another mile?"

I straighten and stretch. "Absolutely. I'm feeling better every day." Meeting Dazaray every morning for a walk did what I thought nothing could—it calmed the negative voices in my head. And jogging? After I got over the embarrassment of being incredibly out of shape, it's something I'm beginning to enjoy.

"I'm so glad I lied to you about being a jogger," I say with a laugh.

She smiles and shrugs. "It's not a lie if you manifest it

into being true."

Mike purrs loudly, rubbing his face back and forth over her chin.

I take a moment to marvel at how one decision can spiderweb change through a person's life. If I didn't impulsively introduce myself to Dazaray I would still be sitting in my apartment alone every day, wondering why my life isn't as I want it to be.

Although Dazaray is also new to the area, she isn't socially awkward like I am. She grew up in the Midwest and I'm pretty sure she never met a person she didn't like. We both work remotely, but she uses her flexible schedule to explore New England.

Will she want to live in Providence next year? She doesn't know. She says she'll go wherever good times, good people, and joy take her. Being with her helps me see that I don't have to overthink everything.

Or waste time wishing I said or did something differently. She believes things work out the way they're meant to, regardless of how we may see ourselves as being in control.

It's that free-thinking side of her that allows me to be real with her. It took a week of walking with her daily for me to confess I never jogged a day in my life. All she did was laugh and tell me nothing happens without a reason. According to her, when I asked her to go for a jog sometime, what I really did was ask the universe to bring healthy habits into my life.

It wasn't a mistake.

Or a lie.

It was my inner self expressing a need and I should honor it.

Two weeks later, I introduced her to Mike and confessed that people in the building thought he was a twenty-five-year-old grad student. She snuggled him, just as she currently is, and announced that Mike must have been brilliant in his past life to choose me and that cover story. I don't know if I agree or disagree with her beliefs, but Mike adores her, so he makes his feelings on the matter clear enough.

Dazaray knows about my prior crush on Greg. I even mentioned Hugh to her and how the two of them met.

There's a lot I didn't tell her about Hugh because . . . well, because even though she's open-minded, I'm still trying to sort truth from fantasy when it comes to him.

Instead of telling her he appeared in my apartment one day, I told her I met him when I least expected to meet anyone. That wasn't a lie.

Rather than saying he believed he fought in World War II, I told her he was old-fashioned.

And Hugh's claim that he somehow become trapped in a fork? I told her he had an incredible imagination and a dry sense of humor.

Where did he go?

I took a page out of Dazaray's book, and since I had no idea of the truth of where he was, I chose a reality I wanted. I said he fell for me and, due to trauma in his past, was overwhelmed and bolted. He'll be back, though, because we are meant to be together.

That's why I kept his clothing.

I prefer this version over the possibility that I slept in the arms of a mentally unstable man and am lucky he didn't confuse me with a Nazi and murder me.

"Do you mind if I have a glass of water before we go?" she asks after putting Mike down.

"Not at all; I need to refill my water bottle too." We head into my kitchen where I retrieve a glass for her and begin to fill it from the spout on the refrigerator.

While waiting, she traces the lettering on the front of the wooden box. "Did this belong to your parents?"

"No, I bought it at an estate sale."

"What is it?"

"Just silverware."

"Can I look at it?"

"Sure."

She opens the lid. "It looks old."

"It is. 1940s."

She picks up a spoon. "My grandparents had a set they received as a wedding present, but it went to my sister. I didn't think I'd ever use it. Do you?"

I shake my head. "Not anymore. You'll probably think I'm crazy, but there was one fork in that set I used all the time. I'm still kind of sad I lost it."

"I get that. I had a hairbrush once that used to make my

hair really shine. Haven't found another that does as well." She takes a closer look at the spoon. "I love old things. I always wonder what they've seen and if they carry any energy from the past with them."

Mike climbs her leg. Dazaray jumps in surprise, drops the spoon and shakes Mike off. "Holy shit, Mike. You scared me."

I place the glass of water on the counter and reach down to pick up the spoon, but before I can, Mike swats it under the refrigerator. "Mike!"

Dazaray is on her knees. "I'll get it." She tilts her head so she can see beneath the fridge. "Mike, you're so naughty, but I think you're about to be forgiven." A second later she's holding up the spoon she'd dropped as well as—

My breath catches in my throat. "My favorite fork."

She hops back to her feet and hands both to me.

I don't care how it looks, I hug the fork to my chest and smile. "I didn't think I'd ever see it again."

"Sometimes the things we think are lost are merely hidden from us until we're meant to have them again." She picks up the glass and takes a long drink then says, "It could be an omen."

"An omen?"

"Of more things coming back to you."

*Hugh.* "I want to believe that."

"Then believe it. Life isn't so much about what happens to us, but rather what we believe is happening. Thoughts shape action, actions shape outcome, therefore thoughts shape outcome."

"Thoughts shape outcome?" A wave of uncertainty washes over me. If that were true, wouldn't Hugh have returned to me the night I purchased a year's supply of condoms and made dinner for him? "I don't know if I believe that. It hasn't been my experience."

"Not believing is like keeping a faucet turned off and wondering why there's no water. Believing comes first." When I don't have an immediate response to that, she asks, "Ready for our jog?"

I nod then return the spoon to its place in the wooden box. I tell myself to put the fork back, but can't seem to force myself to. "Am I crazy if I take the fork with us on the jog?"

"Crazy is a term used by those who choose to limit themselves to what is comfortable for them to believe. Don't ask anyone for permission to be you. Embrace what makes you happy."

A huge smile spreads across my face and I tuck the fork into the side pocket of my running shorts. I never believed in omens, well not good ones, anyway. It was always easier to expect bad things to happen.

What if I didn't look at life that way?

What if I let myself believe in possibilities and happy endings?

*Hugh. Come back to me.*

# Chapter Nineteen

*Mercedes*

*Providence, Rhode Island*
*2024*

LATER IN THE day, after an extra-long jog with Dazaray and several online meetings addressing issues that could have been handled via email, I'm restlessly pacing my living room. After showering I change into the pink dress I bought with Hugh.

Normally, I'd feel silly that I still have it. What do I really know about Hugh? And honestly, how realistic is it to believe he'll come back?

How can believing be enough?

I can't dispute that Dazaray's philosophies improve my life. She got me out of my apartment, into the world, healthier, and I'm even meeting people. She stops and talks to everyone and anyone. I'm not there yet, but the idea of having a conversation with a stranger in line at the store no longer terrifies me.

I even sometimes go out with Greg and his friends. There's no romance there, but they're always happy to see me. He's smarter than he appears. So are his friends. Some are post-grad students and others are research analysts like him.

Last week, they invited me to a casual debate on the ethical and environmental impact of weaponizing mosquitos to reduce diseases in developing countries. My friends back home used to debate which local restaurants had the best half-price happy-hour appetizers. These people read and discuss scientific research—for fun.

Before meeting Dazaray, I would have thought they were gathering for nerdy reasons because better options weren't available. I see now they're unapologetically following their joy.

I intend to do the same.

Follow joy, not the research for fun part.

I want to feel as alive and excited about life as I did with Hugh.

I'm not sure yet what that'll look like.

So far, it's me, alone in a pink dress.

My pacing takes me to the kitchen where my favorite fork is still beside the sink where I left it. I pick it up and look it over, noticing for the first time the imperfection on the back of its handle. The faint line reminds me of the scar on Hugh's back. I chuckle. Talk about coincidences.

Out of curiosity, I look over some of the silverware and note that several of them have small marks on them, all in different areas.

*Because large wounds leave a mark behind when they heal.*

I shake my head and replace the pieces I took out. How much do I want to add excitement to my life? I'm ready to imagine a military unit of men just like Hugh, stuck in some kind of suspended animation right here in my kitchen.

Now, that would be the beginning of an adventure!

I sigh and turn my attention back to the fork Hugh said he was trapped in. How fun would it be to live in a world where magical things like that were possible?

"Are you in there, Hugh?" I whisper.

Nothing.

I turn the fork over and run a finger across the mark on the back of it. As I do, memories of Hugh flood in. I close my eyes and remember how it felt to wake in his arms—the scent and feel of him. His touch. His kiss.

The way he got my humor.

A woman could spend a lifetime with a man who made her feel seen the way Hugh saw me. If only I was brave enough to tell him what I wanted . . .

Giving in to an impulse, I take the fork with me to the living room and place it on the coffee table beside my laptop. *Inkwell.*

I send a text to Greg and ask him if he and his crew are up for helping me research something silly. Within minutes, we're in a Discord chat and I'm lying again. I tell them one of my old uncles told me about his father being part of a secret government super soldier program in World War II . . . code name Inkwell.

I list the names I remember Hugh searching for. I also give them the year Hugh told me he'd joined the program.

**There's no record of a Project Inkwell**, Greg types.

**Because it was top secret**, I respond.

**Everyone on your list died in the United States**, Greg's friend Cheryl writes. She's brilliant. Too smart for Greg to want to date, or so he says. It might be he's not up to her standards. **They all died the same month of the same year. And all in ways that left their bodies difficult to identify. That's odd.**

His friend Leo wrote: **No, that's awesome. Everyone knows that super soldiers must sever ties to their family and friends. What better way to make someone invisible than fake their deaths?**

**I'm going to be up all night now**, Cheryl jokes.

*Me too.*

I look at the fork lying motionless on the table. The likelihood that it is actually connected to Hugh at all is slim—but not zero.

Zero would require the implausible to be impossible and Dazaray would argue that nothing is impossible.

**What did your uncle tell you about the nature of the Inkwell project?** Leo asks.

I share everything I can remember Hugh saying about it.

How they took men who were deemed unfit for the military and injected them with something that gave them special powers. Also, they'd thought their objective was to stop the atomic bomb from being created, by acquiring German scientists for the U.S. government.

Cheryl: **That would be an incredible origin story for a super hero. Classic. Experimented on. Lied to by the government.**

Greg: **Government-made heroes don't live happily ever after. They get unmarked graves when they become a bigger risk than their worth. I hope that's not why we've never heard of them.**

I type: **My uncle said something about them attending an award dinner and then never being seen again. They were in London at the Savoy Hotel.**

**You're so fun**, Cheryl writes. **I love researching stuff like this.**

*Yeah. I know.*

My gaze returns to where the fork is lying on the table. *I don't believe in time travel. I don't think you were ever stuck in a fork. But I believe your search for the truth was sincere.*

*Did you hear about project Inkwell and it haunted you?*

*Haunted.*

*Were you a ghost, Hugh, trying to find your way to the light, asking me to help your story finally be told?*

*If there was a Project Inkwell, my friends will find the truth about it.*

*My friends—I love that I finally have some. Not enough of us for a setting of six, but close.*

*They're smart, Hugh. They'll get you the answers you're looking for.*

*You and your friends won't be forgotten.*

Mike curls up at my side and yawns. Present, but bored.

# Chapter Twenty

*Mercedes*

*Providence, Rhode Island*
*2024*

ANOTHER DAY.

Another early morning jog with Dazaray.

Shower.

Online meetings.

Break for lunch.

I make myself a salad and decide to eat it in the living room while I sort through emails. My laptop is open and I'm ready to dig into both my meal and my workload when I realize I didn't grab a utensil.

As I start to push myself off the couch I spot my favorite fork. It's right there where I left it on the coffee table the night before. I shouldn't be as relieved as I am to have it back in my life, but I feel whole again.

Cradling the fork in one hand, I think about how one

seemingly insignificant decision, dropping by an estate sale for items to fill my new apartment, had such a positive impact on my life.

The words of an old college professor whisper in my thoughts: *Correlation doesn't equal causation.*

That probably does apply in this case.

I bought old silverware.

I met a man who thought he was from the past and claimed to have been trapped in this very fork.

My life improved.

These three events may seem related, but I'm also aware of the principle of Occam's razor, which essentially says that when an event has more than one explanation, the simplest one is most likely the correct one.

So, what's more likely the truth?

That I found a set of magical silverware full of World War II super soldiers, freed one, fell for him, and that journey empowered me to finally take charge of my life?

Or . . .

Did I find old silverware?

Survive an overnight visit from mentally ill man?

And on my own become ready to stop hiding from my life?

Twirling the fork before my face, I shake my head. "I'm not a princess in a fairy tale. I'm a regular woman with a slightly toxic relationship with my parents, a lifetime of anxiety, and a wild imagination." I chuckle with deprecation.

"If you'd stuck around, Hugh, you would have discovered I'd be the perfect romantic partner for a super soldier. No one knows anything about me. I have nerdy friends who could help us discover what happened to you—maybe even set your friends free. I'm loyal, and I have a good amount of money saved because I've worked since my teens and I don't go anywhere or do anything."

Giving in to the fantasy of Hugh being able to hear me, I continue, "I'm also morally gray enough to help you fend off your enemies and never need to confess where we bury the bodies. I don't care how long Greg and I are friends, I'll never tell him we stole his mail—I'm smart enough to know that's the kind of stuff a person should take to their grave." Leaning forward, I stick the fork through some of my salad and lift it to just in front of my mouth. "We could have been a team."

I open my mouth and pause. Although I never saw the fork become Hugh, I also never saw Hugh and the fork at the same time. *Imagine if Hugh isn't gone, or a liar. Imagine if he's this fork again.*

*Not just any fork.*

*My favorite one.*

The salad tastes good, but the fork brings my mouth to life. I've missed it in a way that defies logic.

*Ridiculous.*

*Delicious.*

A bit of dressing sits on the silver above the tines. I lick it away, remembering how Hugh said he knew the taste and feel of me because he'd been in my mouth.

*If you'd come back that night, you would have tasted more than that. So would I.*

My heart begins to race as I remember the feel of his lips on mine. I was ready, so ready, to be his.

*The things I would have done with you . . .*

*To you.* I give in to an impulse and lick the entire length of the fork.

Blame it on the fact I'm in my sexual prime with an embarrassing lack of experience, but I'm so turned on I slide out of my shorts and begin to touch myself. Fork clenched in one hand, fingers of my other hand rubbing back and forth over my clit, I close my eyes and imagine Hugh's head between my legs. He'd kiss my inner thighs before pushing them farther apart and . . .

The fork moves in my hand.

*No, it doesn't.*

*Forks don't move on their own.*

I return my attention to my building pleasure and the fantasy that it's Hugh's tongue loving me instead of my hand. In the past, I considered buying a sex toy, but I wanted my first time to be with someone other than myself.

Now I'm wishing I had a dildo to plunge into me so I could finally feel what it's like to be fucked. I bite my bottom lip and increase my speed, whispering Hugh's name as I do.

This time there's no denying the fork is vibrating in my hand. I should be scared, but my body is already humming with need, and I'm so damn close to a climax I don't want to stop. I turn the fork so the tines are enclosed in my palm and bring its handle to my clit, expecting the metal to be cold, but it's not.

It's warm.

Hard.

And a damn little jackhammer against my clit. Unfucking believable—and so good. I switch hands so I can grip at the cushion while holding the hand with the fork against me.

I spread my legs wider, jutting against the vibrating metal tip, wanting so much more than a fork could ever give me. A wave of pleasure rises in me and I give myself over to the heat that spreads through me.

Eyes still closed, I place the fork next to me on the couch, and enjoy the post orgasm float back to earth. There are perks to having a really good imagination . . . I just fucked myself with a fork and didn't hate it.

When I could be pleased by standards that low, sex with a real man would have to be amazing. Now all I have to do is find one that made me feel anything like Hugh had.

Two strong hands close on my knees and my eyes fly open. *Hugh*.

How did he get in my apartment again?

"Couldn't leave me alone, could you?" he growls. "I told myself I was no good for you, but if this is what you want,

God, it's what I want too." He expertly parts my folds and dives forward, his tongue lashing over me from back to front.

I gasp and try to pull away, but his hands take hold of my hips and he grinds his face into me. Nothing in my life prepared me for the plunge of his tongue inside me. Wet. Hot. Pulsing and swirling.

I had no idea tongues were that big . . . or talented.

All thought of resistance fades when he retracts his tongue, then plunges it into me again. My hands dig into his hair, holding his face to me, as I mindlessly beg for him not to stop.

I've read a fair share of books with oral sex in them, but none of them described anything like this. His tongue whips out and begins a rhythmic dance over my clit that I can only describe as soul-stealing. Back and forth. Circling. Swirling. Tugging.

Just when I think I'm going to come like that, his tongue thrusts inside me, filling me, stretching me, powerfully moving in and out until I can't hold back. My thighs clench around him. Fireworks explode. I'm a shaking, sweaty mess. "Wow."

"Save it, Doll. I'm nowhere near done. Stand up."

I do so, but with his assistance. He strips me bare and runs shaking hands slowly over me like I'm a meal he's waited too long for and is torn between savoring and gulping it down. "Are you truly a virgin?"

Gasping for air, I look up at him. "Are you really here?"

He whips the shirt I bought him over his head and begins to undo his belt. "Answer the question, Mercedes."

I lick my bottom lip. "You first."

He strips naked, tossing the last of his clothing aside. I'm not sure how big the average man is, but when I see the size of his engorged cock I begin to have second thoughts about my first time being with a super soldier—imagined or not. His expression gentles and he runs a hand through my hair. "I'm here, Mercedes. And I'm out of mind for you. I'll do my best to be gentle, but if you don't want this, tell me now."

There's a chance Hugh has really good timing and returned just in time to find me getting off on a fork. Or . . . I glance at the couch beside me. The fork is gone again.

"I don't understand."

He pulls me into his naked embrace and I shudder against him and the extra-large part of him that is pressing against my stomach. "I don't either. I thought I was gone again. I didn't think there was a way back, but then you were there . . . all around me, filling the nothingness with you. There is no me without you, and I'm okay with that. You're the only thing I missed and the only one worth coming back for. I know it's soon, Mercedes, but I can't do this halfway. I want you, not only for today, but for my own, always. Say you feel the same."

How had he gotten back into my apartment? And where had he been? I had so many questions, but I decide to ask them later. I wrap my arms around his bare back and hug him tightly. "I've missed you too."

He takes my hips in his hands and effortlessly lifts me, sliding me up the muscular length of him, until my eyes are level with his. "How long was I gone?"

"Months." Does he really not know? Is that part of his condition? "Why did you leave?"

"I was jealous. Stupid. Angry with myself for not having more to offer you." He shifts my weight and I wrap my legs around his waist. The tip of his cock teases by brushing against my wetness.

"Jealous?" Why am I asking questions when all I really want to do is taste those lips of his again?

"I saw the flowers in the kitchen. Were they from him?"

I strain to remember. "Yes."

His hands clench on my sides. "Did you fuck him?"

I hold his gaze. "No."

Relief floods his eyes and his hold gentles. "Why not?"

I frame his face with my hands. "Because he's not you."

The kiss that follows is deep, frenzied, and so perfect I nearly burst into tears. No one else could compare to him and how he makes me feel matters. When he lifts his head, I whisper, "If you're fucking crazy and need to be institutionalized, I'll get myself diagnosed so we can be together."

He smiles down at me. "What are you talking about?"

"I don't want to do this halfway, either, Hugh. Don't leave me again."

After a pause, he says, "If I ever do, you know how to bring me back."

I shake my head, confused.

He slides a hand between us and a finger into my wet sex. "Put any part of me inside of any part of you . . . that seems to be the magic."

He pumps his finger in and out of me and I'm willing to believe whatever he wants me to as long as he doesn't stop. His breath is hot on my neck as he kisses his way from my ear to my collarbone.

I run my hands over every inch of him I can reach before he bends me backward over his arm and devours my breasts, one after the other. God, everything he does to me unlocks a new level of pleasure.

He smells like heaven.

Tastes like sin.

And I'm ready to belong to him.

"I am a virgin," I whisper in his ear, "but I don't want to be. Can you help me with that?"

He growls a yes while he strides toward my bedroom. With each step, his cock slaps my ass. I can't take it anymore, I want to grab it and shove it inside me.

But Hugh is in no hurry. I can see his plan in his expression when he lays me across my bed and takes his time looking me over, laying claim to me slowly, completely, with his eyes.

"I don't want to hurt you," he says, his nostrils flaring.

"I trust you not to," I answer quietly.

"I can crush a man's skull with my bare hands."

"Let's not do that."

"Right." A smile curls his lips. "They say I have the strength of forty men. I've accidentally thrown someone onto the roof of a building."

"That's strong." I swallow hard. "Maybe you should stop thinking about all the ways this could go wrong and think about how all that strength could be sexy. That's where my mind is going."

"Really?" The grin that spreads across his face brings a smile to mine.

"Yes. Really."

With lightning speed, he's beside me on the bed, rolling me so I'm on top of him. "Ready for a ride?" He slides his hands beneath my thighs and lifts me straight up. I panic and wobble a little, but his hands are large and his grip is sure. "Easy, there, Doll. All you have to do is balance and enjoy."

That sounds easier than it feels. "Okay."

Slowly, he brings me upward until I'm suspended above his face. "I could live here," he murmurs then lowers me onto him. That long tongue of his begins to swirl and plunge. I dig my fingers into my thighs as he laps at my clit, fills me deeply, and teases my backdoor as well. He's everywhere and relentless.

I nearly weep from the loss of his tongue when he lifts

me off his face but only until the tip of his cock brushes at the lips of my sex. I close my eyes and prepare for pain, but he eases just an inch inside of me before lifting me up so he can slide my wet sex along the length of him.

Then I'm above him again, and he's filling me, slightly more this time, and I'm stretching to accommodate the width of him. I want it hard and fast, but I also want it like this. Really, I want whatever he's offering. Another inch and I tense. He's huge.

He moves his hips and his cock is moving within me with the same talent his tongue displayed. I relax and he slides deeper. And deeper. I stretch, but there's no pain. I flex my muscles around the length of him, begging him to go deeper.

He lifts me, brings me back to his face, and plunders me with his tongue all over again—bringing me to the edge of release. I sob when he withdraws his tongue.

All sanity leaves me. I'm all primal need, and when he lowers me onto his cock, I start swearing at him and threatening his life if he doesn't just fuck me.

He thrusts upward, balls deep in me, and I gasp, but it's good . . . so good. Any discomfort I feel is fleeting and overshadowed by how completely he fills me.

Without breaking the connection, he moves to the edge of the bed and stands. I cling to his shoulders. He manipulates my position with the ease of a man who really does have the strength of many.

I can tell he's being careful to not hurt me, but I'm no longer afraid. I meet his thrusts with my own and whisper, "Harder. Faster."

His control snaps and his muscles bulge. Against the wall, I'm ravished by a beast of a man, but the more he takes the more I want to give. I come in a glorious combination of swearing and crying out his name.

He pulls out and pushes me to my knees before him. He doesn't wait for permission and I don't want him to. I open my mouth and he gives no mercy. He fills my mouth so deeply I nearly gag.

"I tasted you so many times, Mercedes. Taste me," he growls.

I open wider for him, lapping at him. He takes my hair tight in his hands, pulling my head back so he can see his cock plunge in and out of my mouth. Every hot scene I read in books pales in comparison to the reality of being taken so completely.

When he comes, I drink him down, and he shudders as he empties into me. He withdraws and lifts me into a feet-dangling hug. "Holy shit, Mercedes. I tried to be gentle. You okay?"

I'd hug him back, but I can't move my arms. All I can do is nod against his chest.

He puts his hands beneath my buttocks and lifts me higher so we're once again eye to eye. "I'm sorry I left the way I did. I didn't know I could, and when I did, I didn't know how to get back."

It's odd and also a huge turn-on to be held before him as if I weigh nothing. Super soldier or not, he's stronger than anyone I ever met. "Where did you go?"

He lowers me to my feet. "Mercedes, I was a fork again."

I wonder if that sounds as crazy to him as it does to me. "I—I know you believe that, but . . ."

He frowns. "You were right here with me when I changed back this time."

I grimace. "I had my eyes closed."

He runs his hand through his hair. "If you don't believe I'm a fork, does that mean you also don't believe I served in World War II?"

My sex is still throbbing from his claiming of it. Every inch of me is warm and tingly in the afterglow of being his. "Do we have to talk about this right now?" I look around, locate my shirt on the floor, and pick it up.

"We do." He removes the shirt from my hand and tosses it back on the floor. "Don't put up walls between us. Tell me the truth. If you don't believe what I've told you, what do you believe?"

I feel uncomfortably exposed, but not because I'm naked. "Whatever the truth is, we'll work with it."

"Whatever the truth is?" He sighs. "You think I'm a liar?"

"No."

"Crazy?"

I chew my bottom lip. "Maybe."

"I don't blame you. This whole situation is insane." He lifts a hand to caress my cheek, and I don't care if he has multiple personalities and this is only one of them. I like him. I like him a lot. "If I try to prove to you that I really am sometimes a fork, will you promise me something?"

He's looking down at me like I'm the only woman he ever or could ever want, and I don't have the strength to deny him. "Anything."

"If you have to fuck me again to bring me back . . . do it."

"That's an easy promise to make."

"No matter what form I'm in."

Oh, my God, he really thinks he can turn into a fork. What will he do when he realizes he can't? Will that cause a psychotic break? "You don't have to prove anything to me, Hugh."

"I do and that's okay." He makes a face.

Grunts.

Makes another painful face.

Grunts again.

"Do you need the bathroom?" I ask. He looks like he's trying to push something out.

His hands fist and he brings them to the sides of his head. "Why can't I fucking do this? Why can't I ever get anything right?"

And then, right before my eyes, with a hazy burst of

light, he disappears and a fork, my favorite fork, falls to the floor.

Oh, my God, he really is a fork.

My fork.

I fucked my fork.

I was forked.

I rush to my knees beside him. "Hugh, I'm sorry I didn't believe you. Come back."

Nothing.

I pick him up and cradle him between my bare breasts. "Don't you dare leave me now. Hugh . . . can you hear me?"

Nothing.

"Vibrate if you can hear me."

Now what do I do?

This is all my fault.

He told me he wasn't sure he knew how to get back. What did he ask me to do? Fuck him to bring him back?

How?

I blush as I remember how I used the handle of the fork to orgasm earlier. "Okay. Okay. If that's what it takes."

I pick Hugh up and carry him to the bed. The idea of using a fork after I was with Hugh wasn't tempting.

*But this* is *Hugh.*

I lie back on the bed and place the handle to my clit. It doesn't move.

Oh, no.

I rub it back and forth over my nub. "Hugh, I know

you're in there. Come back. Come back to me."

It's not working.

I close my eyes and imagine Hugh touching me instead of the fork. I whisper his name over and over, all while moving his handle back and forth. Images of Hugh fill my thoughts. I writhe against the warming metal.

The fork begins to vibrate.

*Hugh* begins to vibrate.

"Come on, Hugh. You can do it. You can do me again if you get your ass back here."

And just like that, metal is replaced by a talented, wet tongue . . .

# Chapter Twenty-One

*Mercedes*

*Rhode Island*
*2024*

LATER, LYING IN Hugh's arms beneath a comforter on my bed, I trace the strong muscles of his chest. I'm sore, but sated. "Hugh?"

"Yes?" he murmurs and kisses my forehead.

"You're a fork."

His chest vibrates with a chuckle. "Sometimes."

"Everything you said about being a super soldier is true."

"Yes."

"I'm going to find out what happened to you and your friends at that award ceremony." I pause, then confess. "Actually Greg and his friends will. I've already put the challenge before them."

His hand tightens possessively on my bare bottom. "Greg?"

I love the intense look in his eyes. I want to be his and his alone. "We're friends now. And his friends are some of the smartest people I ever met. If anyone can solve this mystery, they can."

"Just friends?"

"Yes."

He inhales deeply. "Who gave you the flowers?"

"He did. I laid them by the sink because I was headed out to the pharmacy."

"Why?"

His eyes darken as I tell him what I planned for that evening and how I not only bought condoms, but lingerie, and even made him a meal. "I should have waited and asked you about the flowers."

I shrug. "We were still getting to know each other. I'm still adjusting to you being both real and a fork."

He tips my head up to look into my eyes. "Why were you willing to be with me if you thought I was delusional?"

I hold back the defensive jokes that come to mind. My life is what I choose to make it and I'm choosing to be less judgmental of myself. "When you say it like that it sounds bad. I always was a little odd. No one like you ever gave me a second look . . ."

He kisses away the rest of what I would have said, then hugs me tightly. "I know how it is to feel like you're not enough. I traded everything for the chance to be more. Was it worth it? Losing my parents, my friends, all control over who I am? Not if I still hate myself."

I inhale deeply. "I moved away from everything and everyone I knew because I hoped I'd be different if my location was. All that changed was my zip code." Splaying a hand across his chest, I say, "Until you."

His eyes smile at me. "And what did I do?"

I tell him about how meeting him set me on a path of being braver and how that led to meeting Dazaray. "Even becoming friends with Greg and his circle wasn't possible before you. I needed to start seeing myself as someone interesting enough for someone to want to be with. If you can do that for me, maybe I can be your catalyst to start liking yourself."

He kisses my forehead. "I only need to know I did one damn thing right."

I push myself onto one elbow and feel surprisingly confident for once. "I refuse to believe we can only be what we always were. Whatever you did in the past doesn't define you. There's a reason you're still here. You were given a second chance to make a difference. What you decide to do with it—that's who you are."

He rolls me beneath him and smiles at me. "I like the way you see the world and who I am with you."

No one ever said that or looked straight into my soul the way he does. We feel meant to be. "Same," I say breathlessly.

"You sure you want to be with a fork?" There's a vulnerability to him that melts my heart.

"It's too late to ask myself that." I trace the side of his face. "I'm already forked."

He laughs and groans. "You went there."

I laugh along shamelessly, feeling young, free, and sexy beneath him. "I did and I'd do it again."

With a serious expression, he says, "You need to know that sometimes, when I'm asleep, I change color to match the pattern of my blanket."

"If I have cheese I fart so loud it wakes me up."

He barks out a laugh.

I shrug and wrinkle my nose at him. "I thought we were sharing our secrets."

He rolls again, pulling me with him and cuddles me to his side. "Mercedes, does nothing shock you?"

I bury my face in his shoulder, breathe in the scent of him, and smile before answering. "I was just intimate with a utensil to help you shape-shift. Do you really think seeing your skin take on a plaid design could compare to that?"

"I guess not."

"Do you have any other powers?"

"I wouldn't call that a power."

"Whatever, you know what I mean. What else can you do?"

He takes a moment to think about it. "I'm not only stronger, but I can stretch more. Not long distances, but I seem to be able to make parts of my body larger or smaller."

"Which parts?"

"My arms and legs."

I swallow hard. "Oh, I think more than that."

He cocks his head at me. "What?"

"I'm not complaining." I blush. "But I don't think everyone's tongue can do what yours does."

His eyes spark with understanding then humor. "Now I'm intrigued." His grin is pure temptation. "Get some rest. We'll explore this more tomorrow."

I warm all over and melt against him. "Hugh?"

He nuzzles my neck. "Hmm?"

"Please be here when I wake."

Holding me tighter, he tenses. "I'm not going anywhere."

*Not if I can help it.*

He doesn't say those last words aloud, but I hear them. He can't promise me he won't leave me again, because he doesn't fully understand what's going on.

I don't either.

I don't understand what happened to him, why being intimate with me frees him . . . any of it.

What did the government do to him?

I wish I was smart enough to promise to figure it out, but I almost didn't graduate from college. I'm not stupid, but I'm easily distracted. That's why I chose to work remotely. I get my work done, but on my schedule and with as many breaks as I need.

I'm good at gathering resources and connecting like-minded people, but in a life-or-death situation, could I correctly fill out a blank map of the United States? Meh. I could do the perimeter states, but the middle ones?

I don't want to brag, but I am really good at locating Montana ever since someone told me it looks like it's sniffing Idaho. Check it out. You'll never confuse that state again.

Hugh deserves better than me.

Dazaray says everything happens for a reason.

*Is that true?*

All I know for sure is that I'm falling in love with a fork.

# Chapter Twenty-Two

*Hugh*

*Providence, Rhode Island*
*2024*

I WAKE TO Mike, sitting on my chest, tapping my forehead with one paw. He meows silently. Our eyes meet and it feels like a pivotal moment in our relationship. "I know it was you who shoved me under the refrigerator."

He holds my gaze, bringing his paw to his mouth as if the need to clean my scent off it is greater than his guilt. His expression when he lowers his paw says, *I'd do it again.*

"I care about her," I say. "A lot. I wish we met under better circumstances, but she's the only part of all of this that makes sense to me. So, glare at me all you want, I'm here for as long as she'll have me."

Unimpressed, Mike circles and flicks my face with his tail before hopping off the bed and leaving the room. I wish it were as possible for me to walk away from everything that

I don't like.

Until last night, that included myself.

Mercedes not only revs my engine, she gives me hope.

I can start over.

And, this time, I can get things right.

I kiss her cheek, slip out of bed, and step into a pair of shorts. After a quick bathroom visit, I head to the kitchen to feed my growling stomach.

The coffee maker is different than the ones I'm used to, but like everything else I encountered so far . . . it is easy enough to figure out how to use. The stove is similar—more buttons and displays, but not as amazing as one would think a future stove would be.

I make a pot of coffee and a large stack of pancakes, then set the table for two. Mercedes walks in the room dressed in the shirt I wore the day before.

Never has a woman taken my breath away the way she does. My shirt covers her to mid-thigh and should be modest enough, but her nipples are budding visibly, and I never found a pin-up more beautiful.

Her face flushes with delight when she sees that I made breakfast for us, and my heart does a little flip. It takes so little to make her happy. I want to punch every man she met before me for not treating her better—but I'm also glad they were too blind to have her first.

She's mine.

All mine.

I put my arms out and, with the speed and power of Thor's hammer, she flies to me. That moment changes me—heals me in a way I could never put into words. With her, I don't feel lost or powerless.

She's why I'm still here and wherever that makes us, feels meant to be. I lift her, spin her, then try to convey my feelings for her in a kiss that leaves us both panting and shaking. "I was about to come wake you."

She searches my face, tears filling her eyes. "This is real. You're real. And you're still here. I wasn't sure you would be."

I hug her to me, tucking her beneath my chin. The mistakes I made are nearly a century in the past. I can't change what I did back then. There's no one alive left to apologize to, even if I wanted to. I'm taking Mercedes's advice and from this moment on I'll be the man I should have been all along. I can do better. I *will* do better. "I told you I'm not going anywhere. Except back to my hometown briefly if you'd like to go for a drive today."

She tips her head back. "Where are you from?"

"Mendon, Massachusetts. My parents owned a small farm there. When I joined the program, it was on the condition that I agreed to sever all contact with my family and anyone who knew me. I was too eager to go and fight to understand what that might mean, but I did ask my sister to do something for me."

"What?"

"My father served in World War I and was a coin collector. He came back with several coins he said I should hold on to because they'd be worth something. I told my sister that if anything happened to me, she should bury them next to the tree where we buried my favorite dog. I told her to never tell anyone, because I'd be back for them. She said what I was asking her to do didn't make sense, but she'd do it anyway."

"That's beautiful . . . and so sad."

I smile down at Mercedes. "If she didn't do it, I'm going to kick her ass . . . or her grandchildren, if I can find them."

She gives me a long look. "Where did you get the money you left in my kitchen?"

"In something called a cage fight."

Her mouth rounds. "You could have been hurt!"

"I was hurt." I hold up my finger with the white line. "But I heal, remember?"

"So you're . . . immortal?"

"Hardly. I'm aging normally so I assume I'll have a natural lifespan. However, as long as I'm not dead, I heal and only the large wounds leave scars."

"You *really* are a superhero."

My laugh is ironic. "Mercedes, don't build me up into more than I am. I'm just a man who wanted to do something important and ended up not making a difference at all. The 'gifts' the government gave me? The only person they saved was me in the end and I'm not sure I deserve to still be here."

"Do you know who says things like that?"

I shake my head.

"Superheroes." Her smile is adorably infectious.

We kiss then I nuzzle her neck. "Thank you for seeing good in me even when I'm struggling to."

She hugs me so tight I can barely breathe. "You're going to be okay, Hugh. I'll help you."

Our gaze meets again. "You're going to be okay too, Mercedes. You're not alone anymore. You have me."

I catch a glimpse of the Inkwell box and stop the negative thoughts as soon as they begin. Like Mercedes, I need to stop looking down. Just because things are difficult doesn't mean they're impossible. "Mercedes, I was a good son. I tried to be a good soldier. But I was never in control of what happened to me. The first time I turned into a fork was something done to me. The second time, I chose the nothingness because it felt like it was all I had. The third time, I chose it to prove something to you. If I can choose to be a fork, why can't I choose to come back?"

"I don't know, Hugh, but I promise I'll help you figure that out." She wrinkles her nose at me. "Even if it means you won't need me anymore."

I'll always need her. She's what was missing in me. Some things are better shown with actions rather than words. I pick Mercedes up, toss her over my shoulder, and head toward the bedroom.

Laughing, she asks, "What are you doing?"

"I'm going to fuck you until you stop doubting how I feel about you."

She shudders and says breathlessly, "You know who says things like that?"

"Who?"

"*My* superhero."

# Chapter Twenty-Three

*Mercedes*

*Providence, Rhode Island*
*Weeks later*

I'M TRYING TO concentrate on answering work emails, but I can't stop sneaking looks at Hugh. Beside me on the couch, his attention is focused on the new laptop we bought with some of the money he won from the cage fight.

He looks up, catches me watching him, and gives my forehead a kiss before returning to the spreadsheet he's creating. We've had more sex in the past few weeks than some people probably have in their entire lives. I added inexhaustible sexual stamina to his list of superpowers.

With a sated sigh, I add kindness and loyalty to that list as well. He seems to have an endless supply of those. I smile as I remember what he said when I told him that. His response had been a simple, "With you."

No one ever made me feel so good about being myself. I

love being part of Hugh's journey from a confused and disheartened soldier to a hopeful man with a purpose. He has taken to technology like someone born in the age of it.

Right now, he's researching auctions where he can sell the coins we dug up from a wooded area that used to be his family's farm. We paid someone to create a digital ID for him then opened a bank account together.

Together.

I'm not alone anymore, and every day is better than the one before.

*Hugh Michael Wilson . . .* That's the name we decided on. Wilson was his grandfather's first name. And the middle name? Mike had walked away in a huff when we told him we were naming Hugh after him. Nothing makes Mike happy, not since he was neutered.

Life is good.

Hugh is incredible.

Not perfect. No man is. He's stubborn. After two weeks together, he decided he should meet my parents. I suggested we wait until he has full control over when he changes into a fork. My parents are open-minded . . . but I don't want to explain that side of our relationship to them.

He argued that he didn't feel right about living with me without at least looking my father in the eye, shaking his hand, and promising to take care of me. I probably shouldn't have told him that was an outdated practice.

He folded his arms across his chest and clattered to the

floor in fork form. Arguing with Hugh would be easier if he could change himself back. We've been experimenting with his shapeshifting, but so far, he can't.

His first transformation happened simply from him being in my mouth. We tried that, but it wasn't enough. I have to not only be intimate with him, I have to be yearning for him.

That can be difficult in the middle of a disagreement, so the day we argued about my parents, I put Hugh on the counter, went for a jog with Dazaray, returned, and only then brought him back.

Don't even feel bad for him. He totally milks the whole "I can't revert back unless you're intimate with me" thing. Sometimes he'll look me in the eye, wiggle his eyebrows playfully and BING he's a vibrating fork again. The little stinker.

I don't actually mind. Once or twice, I may have argued with him over something I didn't care about just to see if I could get him to change. The twinkle in his eye right before I succeeded, told me he knew what I was doing and it's become a little game for us.

I definitely can't take him home to meet my parents yet.

If I didn't think it would attract the attention of whatever government agency had recruited him, I would do one of those "Am I the asshole?" TikToks.

Hugh and I went to dinner the other night. We had the world's slowest waiter. I'm pretty sure he drove home between coming over to ask for our drink order and delivering them. I was starving. It was only after the waiter dropped off our food and disappeared again that we realized he'd forgotten to give us silverware.

I looked at Hugh.

He looked at me.

I gave him puppy dog eyes. Some of my humanity leaves when I'm really hungry.

He went home in my purse and later we laughed about it. We're following our joy together and life is better than I ever thought it could be.

That doesn't mean we've put aside our responsibilities.

Both Hugh and I are still dedicated to finding out what happened to his unit, we just choose to not be miserable while we solve that puzzle.

Hugh entertains my fantasy of him as a superhero and together we're exploring his special gifts—in and out of the bedroom. His ability to stretch and enlarge? Lord, he can't ever leave me because I'm ruined for all other men.

With practice, he's learning to control his camouflaging abilities. He's only difficult to find when naked, but that makes the games we play more fun. I got over feeling awkward about loving a fork. And, although I don't want to be intimate with any other silverware, I did offer to do whatever was necessary to free his friends. He said we'd find another way.

*Thank God.*

Hugh's old-fashioned and faithful. None of that sounds as sexy as it is, but he's devoted to taking care of me in a way modern men never offered to. I feel not only safe with him, but treasured. "I forking love you."

He barks out a laugh, then puts his laptop down before taking mine from me and putting it to the side as well. Lifting me with ease, he moves me from beside him on the couch to straddling his jean-clad lap. My sundress flutters around us like an upside-down flower opening for him. "I forking love you too, Mercedes. One day soon, you'll be Mrs. Hugh Wilson."

I run my hands over his strong chest and grind my sex over his hardening shaft. "Are you asking me to marry you?"

He slips both hands beneath my dress, cups my ass and moves his hips back and forth against me. I bite my lips as my body heats and readies for his. "Who's asking? You're mine, Mercedes. Today. Tomorrow. Forever."

"For better or for worse," I say with a smile.

"Till death do us part," he continues with so much love in his eyes I nearly die right then.

*Yes.*

A thought comes to me, and I voice it without thinking. "Can we have children? Would that be safe? Would I be birthing cutlery?"

My question takes him by surprise, and he looks genuinely concerned, then he smiles. "If so, I hope we have a spoon."

"Jerk." I smack his chest playfully. "You could have just said you don't know."

I get it, though. There's no way *to* know and laughing is how he deals. I'm learning to do the same. It's better than hiding.

My phone buzzes with a text. I check it. "It's Cheryl. She's still researching Inkwell."

He tenses beneath me. "Did she find anything?"

I text that question to her then read her response. "She asked me if my uncle is still alive. She has some leads she'd like to follow up on, but she wishes she had more information."

Hugh's lips purse. "If it'll help my friends, I'll tell her whatever I know."

"I told her it was my uncle who told me about Inkwell. Who would I say you are?"

"We might have to be honest with her."

My breath catches. "How honest?"

"Is she single?"

I frown. "Why?"

He taps my nose gently. "Not for me. But if she doesn't have a man in her life and is open-minded, you could lend her a spoon."

## The End for Now . . .

For more about what happened at the award dinner and to meet another super soldier read *Spooned*: **A lighthearted utensil romance, book 2 (Jack).**

And because cutlery is always best when it comes in a set, **Knifed: A lighthearted utensil romance, book 3** will round off the series with a bad boy (Ray).

Enjoy my sense of humor? I'm known for my sweet but spicy billionaire series. Start with *Maid for the Billionaire*; it has all the escapism romance and humor without the cutlery. It's binge reading at its best with more than 40 stand-alone books set in the same billionaire world.

# About the Author

Ruth Cardello was born the youngest of 11 children in a small city in southern Massachusetts. She spent her young adult years moving as far away as she could from her large extended family. She lived in Boston, Paris, Orlando, New York—then came full circle and moved back to New England. She now happily lives one town over from the one she was born in. For her, family trumped the warmer weather and international scene.

She was an educator for 20 years, the last 11 as a kindergarten teacher. When her school district began cutting jobs, Ruth turned a serious eye toward her second love—writing and has never been happier. When she's not writing, you can find her chasing her children around her small farm, riding her horses, or connecting with her readers online.

## Contact Ruth:

Website: RuthCardello.com
Email: RCardello@RuthCardello.com
FaceBook: Author Ruth Cardello
Twitter: @RuthieCardello

Made in United States
North Haven, CT
11 December 2024

62217286R00095